Maggie O'

Seven Years Forgotten

Judy,

Hope you enjoy

Maggie O' and her

adventures.
Pamela Boleyn

Pamela Boleyn

Boleyn Books

ISBN: 9781707559442

V-FV5

To contact the author:

Boleyn Books
P. O. Box 382
Daphne, Alabama 36526

www.BoleynBooks.com

CONTENTS

Maggie O'

Seven Years Forgotten

PAMELA BOLEYN

CHAPTER ONE

AFTER THE ACCIDENT

People here tell me it's Monday, March 16, 2015. I feel like Sleeping Beauty, having slept for seven years; only I'm disappointed that a handsome prince didn't wake me. Even a handsome non-prince would improve this situation. My best friend, Mary, tells me that I live in Gulf Shores, Alabama, and that I'm thirty-two years old. I'll give them a couple of weeks to help me sort this out--then I'm going home, wherever that may be. Hell, I might as well start my life over in Italy, for that matter, like that woman in that movie, Under the Tuscan Sun. I'm so glad Mary flew from New York City with me to Santa Rosa. She looks older than I remember her.

"Hey, Maggie, I hope you slept well."

"Not really. For the price of a stay here, they should up their standards. Hampton Inns are far better than this. I need a prostitute's breakfast."

"What on Earth is that?"

"Mary, you're so naïve, a large cup of coffee and two cigarettes."

"Maggie, you haven't smoked since college."

"I started again when I got my divorce. I just didn't want anybody to know it."

Mary handed her some folded garments. "I brought you some clothes to wear."

Maggie held up a light green scrub top. "Did you borrow these scrubs from Grey's Anatomy?"

3

"They have a conservative dress code; nothing you brought is acceptable. You can wear my extra sweater. Even thought we're in California it's still a bit nippy. Now get dressed."

After breakfast, Mary took Maggie to a conference room in the main building. Sitting at the conference table were Dr. Roberts, with whom Maggie had already spoken on the phone, and Dr. Jim, whom she had met when she checked in. Both stood up as she entered. Dr. Roberts walked over to her with his hand extended, briefly shook her hand, and began speaking.

"Maggie, please have a seat. I would like to ask you some general questions about yourself. If you don't know an answer, that's fine; this isn't a graded assignment."

"I'm glad to know that since I didn't have a chance to study, or did I?"

Dr. Jim chuckled at her remark. Maggie found him quite attractive. He appeared to be single, not wearing a ring, probably in his early thirties.

Dr. Roberts looked in his mid-forties, wore a wedding ring, and had premature gray hair. "Maggie, please tell us what you remember about yourself."

"I don't know why I was in New York; I live in Atlanta. I'm recently divorced and work as a credit analyst at Wells Fargo Bank. I also volunteer at the High Museum of Art."

Dr. Roberts said, "Tell us about your family."

"My mother lives in Birmingham, and my dad lives in Santa Fe with his third wife, Patty. They just had a son they named, Colin."

"Where did you go to college, and what did you study?"

"University of Alabama. I had a double major in Finance and Art."

"Are you dating anyone right now?"

"No." I don't think occasionally sleeping with Ron should count.

Dr. Jim took over the questioning. "Maggie, why did you get divorced?"

Maggie looked into Dr. Jim's clear blue eyes and replied, "He got one of his classmates pregnant."

Dr. Jim replied, "That must've hurt you. I'm truly sorry. Maggie, I understand you're a gifted artist. Tell me about some of your paintings?"

"I really haven't painted since I was at Alabama. Ron, my art professor, encouraged me to go the academic route and get an MFA at SCAD, that's Savannah College of Art and Design. My mother pressured me to get married."

Dr. Jim smiled at her. "My partner, Steve, graduated from SCAD."

Maggie smiled back, "Small world."

"Yes, it certainly is. So, you don't remember living in Chicago or moving back to Gulf Shores?"

"I don't have a clue what you're talking about. May I ask you a question, Dr. Jim?"

"Of course."

"Why was I living in Chicago?"

"You were living with a friend there."

Maggie had a quizzical look on her face. "And who was I living with?"

"Someone you'd met and dated in Atlanta."

Maggie slammed her hand down on the conference table. "This is truly maddening. Will I ever be able to recall what happened?"

Dr. Roberts said, "Maggie, we're hopeful that you will. But sometimes it takes a while."

"I'd like to learn more about this type of amnesia I have; could I do some research?"

Dr. Roberts hesitated before he replied, "Not during your initial treatment."

"Why? Are you afraid I might find out who I really am?"

Dr. Jim spoke up, "Right now you're still fragile, and we don't want anything to cause you to regress."

Dr. Roberts added, "We don't want you overloaded with too much information at once. It would be way more than you could handle at this point--emotionally. Maggie, when you came to at Matthew's apartment, was anything familiar to you?"

"Oddly, there was a beautiful red dress that was hanging up in his closet. Mary said it belonged to me. Also, I was wearing an unusual ring; when I checked in here, they asked me to take it off. Mary is keeping it for me."

Dr. Jim said, "Do you know who gave you the ring?"

Maggie shook her head no. "There was something special about it. I wondered if it belonged to one of my grandmothers. Oddly though, I was wearing it on my left hand."

Dr. Roberts said, "Maggie can you tell us what you remember about any past sexual relationship you were involved in?"

Miffed by his prying question, she replied, "What do you want me to do, start running down the list of all the guys I've slept with? You only have me scheduled for an hour, right?"

Dr. Jim interjected, "You don't need to give us much detail, just a general overview, like when you lost your virginity."

Maggie defiantly stood up, crossing her arms. "You know, I agreed to come here because I can't remember the last seven years of my life. I don't think my years before that are any of your business."

CHAPTER TWO

BEFORE THE ACCIDENT

As the MD-80 jet pulled back from the gate at Pensacola Airport, Maggie removed a handwritten note stowed inside her *ARTnews* magazine. The embossed cotton fiber paper rattled in her trembling hands. Lifting it to her nose she inhaled its scent. *He still remembers how I love lavender.* The yearning for Chris's special touch consumed her soul once again. Their brief affair the summer before her college freshman year ended a dozen years ago. She had saved her virginity for him, and in return he had broken his promise to her.

As the plane lifted towards the cloud filled morning sky, Maggie clawed at the armrests of her front row aisle seat. She always sat in the seat closest to the Emergency Exit. Within several minutes of the ascent, she felt light-headed, trying to catch her breath; the Xanax had not kicked in. Grabbing an airsickness bag, she exhaled into it. To Maggie it felt like an eternity before the pilot turned off the Fasten Seatbelt sign. Quickly unbuckling her seatbelt, she rushed forward to the first class toilet. Maggie pulled her unruly auburn hair into a low ponytail, patted her rose-flushed face with a wet paper towel, and then scrutinized herself in the mirror. *Get a hold of yourself.* After using a diaphragmatic breathing technique to help calm her anxiety, she returned to her seat.

An elderly woman, sitting across the aisle from her asked, "Dear, are you okay?"

The sweet woman's mannerisms reminded Maggie of her

endearing Grandmother Mona. How much she missed her grandmother, taken away from her in a fatal automobile accident.

Maggie forced herself to smile back. "I'm just afraid of heights."

"I have a son in Seattle who's the same way. He refuses to fly, so he rarely comes to visit me. My name is Rose Anderson."

More relaxed, Maggie said. "Nice to meet you, Rose. I'm Maggie O'Reilly."

"That's a beautiful Irish name; where are you from?"

"Gulf Shores. And you?"

"Pensacola. I'm going to see my first great-grandchild in Atlanta. I'm guessing my granddaughter must be around your age; she's twenty-six. She just had a baby girl, named after me."

"You must be proud. I'm a bit older."

"No children?"

Maggie had just turned thirty-one. Most of her Phi Pi sisters were already settled down in committed relationships, and several had started their families. While attracting men like a magnet, she could never keep them. She felt like an empty glass of ice waiting to be filled with bourbon.

Maggie shook her head, no, and replied with a slight smile, "Rose, if you don't mind, I'm feeling a little drowsy. I might try and rest before we land."

Before closing her eyes she pulled up her sweater sleeve and brushed her fingertips across her left forearm; the scars were faintly visible. The urge to cut returned. She couldn't stop thinking about that sultry July morning at the family beach cottage that led to her first experience with self-injury. She vividly recalled piercing her finger with her grandfather's pocketknife, then gazing at the droplets of crimson blood. How much she still despised her deceased mother, Wanda.

John Kramer impatiently waited at the departure gate, reviewing a new investment proposal. His flight to New York was delayed. It agitated him that the estimated departure time was not yet posted. His firm should go ahead and purchase a private jet, so he wouldn't be wasting his time like this. He had important business to deal with in New York, negotiating the sale of a biotech company that his venture capital fund had invested in five years earlier. The deal would add millions to John's already impressive bank account. But it wasn't about the money anymore; he was addicted to the high stakes involved in the venture capital business. Once he set his mind to a challenge, he became obsessed, immersing himself and shutting out everything around him.

Glancing up from his laptop, he could not help but stare at a beguiling redhead, swaying her hips as she approached him. Dressed in an unbuttoned red wool trench coat, she looked like she just tumbled out of bed. Her face radiated a natural-earthy glow that showed off her fair complexion, her amazing high cheekbones, long neck, green killer eyes, and her delicious full lips. She had an uncanny resemblance to Ruby, who was his deceased mother's best friend and the woman who took his virginity.

After three divorces, he had limited his carnal pleasure to escapades during his frequent business trips to Hong Kong and Singapore. There, women were totally attentive to his needs, leaving him no fear of plans for an attachment afterwards. But seeing this enchanting redhead had dangerously lifted the crotch of his charcoal gabardine pants.

Maggie arrived at the gate just as the Delta agent announce that Flight 211 to New York had been delayed. She found an end seat and placed her carry-on bag on the floor next to her. As she slipped out of her coat, she sensed eyes on her from across the aisle. The not-unattractive man looked her up and down. His bespectacled-framed eyes, lingered on the tight black cashmere that stretched thin over her braless breasts. She removed her ponytail holder and shook her head slightly so that her auburn mane spilled over her shoulders, just stopping before her pinnacle-shaped breasts. She crossed her lanky legs. The right toe of her black leather boot aimed directly towards him, while her tobacco suede skirt hiked up two inches above her bare right crossed knee. Out of a nervous habit, she started dangling her right foot.

It had been a while since she had wanted a man to notice her. After her dismal breakup with Sean, she had filled the void with one-night stands until she had reached a saturation point, and adopted a celibate lifestyle. Something about this alluring stranger caused a stirring inside her. She recognized the plumage he wore, having dated a previous peacock, whom also dressed in the finest menswear. He looked intriguing, possibly an executive, investor, or lawyer. He was not wearing a wedding band, but men often hid them when they wished to attract a willing female. She guessed he was in his mid-forties, the perfect age when a man knows what he wants in life and has acquired the entire arsenal to obtain it.

Maggie took off her silk black and white houndstooth scarf and leaned over her bag. Her sweater's plunging neckline allowed her voyeur to see a tantalizing view, as she rummaged through her bag. She panicked, thinking she had left the book on the previous plane. The Delta representative announced an unexpected blizzard in New York had caused her flight to be cancelled.

Maggie looked up and noticed the stranger, absorbed on his laptop, had turned away. She wondered what his plans might be and *if* his final destination was also New York. Was it business travel, or was he headed home to a wife, girlfriend, or mistress?

Airports imitate our lives; you're either arriving or departing from another place, taking baggage with you along the way. Maggie wished she could lose the baggage she had collected from her own life.

A minute later, John removed his Oliver Peeples eyeglasses and stared intensely across to her. He lifted his thick wiry brows as he said, "According to the weather report, we'll be lucky to get out tomorrow."

Maggie noticed a slight scar trailing up his cheek that drew attention to his deep baby blue eyes and lent an aura of mystery and danger to his appearance. Admiring his sun-streaked chestnut hair brushed back, Maggie was drawn to his chiseled jawline and cheekbones. She wanted to grab him by his Burberry red tie and press her lips against his firmly set mouth, which had probably kissed more than his fair share of women.

Maggie retrieved her houndstooth scarf and draped it around her neck. As she stood up holding her coat and carry-on, she said, "I hate layovers. Guess I'll check into an airport hotel."

"I know a much better place."

Intrigued, she responded to him, "Where?"

"Trust me, you'll like it."

Maggie had finished her phone call, cancelling her first night stay in New York, when her newfound stranger asked, "Where are you staying in New York?"

"The Surrey."

As they rolled their carry-on bags onto the jam-packed airport train, he continued his inquisition. "Why are you headed to New York?"

Looking up his towering frame, she asked, "I wanted to ask the same question of you. I'm a partner in The Launch art gallery in SoHo." She liked how he continued to look directly into her eyes and gave her a warm smile.

11

"You must deal with high-end art to be staying at The Surrey."

Maggie couldn't help but laugh. "Fortunately, I don't have to support myself. My grandparents set up a trust fund for me."

"Let's continue this conversation in the limo."

John had called the owner of a private limo service to pick them up. Maggie would learn that the sixty-seven year-old black driver was also a deacon at the Gospel Baptist Church. A recent widower, he was the most eligible bachelor of his largely elderly congregation.

"Good afternoon, Mr. Kramer. Sorry about your flight."

"Samuel, this is Miss…"

He awkwardly turned to Maggie and said, "I'm sorry, we never formally introduced ourselves."

"I'm Maggie O'Reilly."

She extended her hand, and John pressed his lips against it, while staring into Maggie's magnetic green eyes. "It's a pleasure to meet you, Maggie. I'm John Kramer. Turning he said, "Samuel, Miss O'Reilly and I need a ride to the downtown Ritz."

Feeling chilled, Maggie put her coat back on leaving it unbuttoned. Samuel grinned at Maggie, showing off his gold-capped front tooth. "Let me help you with your bag, Miss O'Reilly."

"Thank you, Samuel. I must get your business card. I come to Atlanta often and I hate driving in the traffic."

As Samuel's limo headed downtown, the late afternoon sun was blocked by the gray and overcast sky. It looked as though it was preparing to snow or sleet, depending on how much further the temperature dropped.

John continued his questions. "Tell me more about your business."

"Besides exhibiting our artist's work, we consult with them on the best ways to market their art. We're like an incubator for them."

"Do they pay you for that?"

"No. These clients are typically your starving artists. We become their agent, and represent them even after they move on to larger galleries. We want them to move on; we make more money as their work becomes more widely known."

"What an interesting business model. Do you have a business background?"

"A double major in Art and Finance."

"That's an unusual combination."

"I couldn't decide which side of my brain I wanted to use. My left brain won when I got a real job working in commercial banking. Why are you headed to New York?"

"I'm a venture capitalist from San Francisco; we have an office in New York."

"I adore San Francisco. I have a friend who lives in Rutherford. When I see her, I try to spend at least one night in San Francisco."

"With your lovely Southern accent, you must be from around here."

"I'm originally from Birmingham. Now, I live in Gulf Shores on the Alabama coast."

"I don't see a ring. Is there a Mr, O'Reilly?"

"I took back my maiden name after I divorced. My ex wanted a bloodline heir. He got what he wanted; he knocked up another medical student." Maggie shook her head in disbelief; she had been telling this stranger her life story. "I'm running off at the mouth, a bad habit of mine. It's my turn to ask you a question."

"Ask me anything."

"You have investigated my marital status; do I need to be concerned with yours?"

"Do you want to know if I'm married?"

"I'm sure you're married."

"Why do you assume that?"

"I just took a chance and guessed."

Maggie found his eyes penetrating, as though he were capable of reading between the lines. It seemed he knew her past and future--as well as her thoughts.

"Do you take chances often, like you are doing now, riding in a limo with a stranger going to a hotel?"

"I like playing games of chance. Don't you?"

As the limo pulled up to the Ritz Carlton entrance, John said, "I hope this is acceptable."

"I've never stayed at this Ritz location."

John winked at Samuel as he paid him. "Samuel, I'll call you to arrange our ride back to the airport."

It was almost five o'clock when Maggie and John entered the contemporary embellished lobby. As she admired the edgy modern décor, John said, "Check out the art collection while I check in."

Maggie pulled out her Amex card and pointed it towards John, "Use this for my room."

He refused her card and said, "You can't do that."

"Why not?"

John smiled "Because I've abducted you."

Taken off guard by his remark, Maggie returned his smile and replied, "Not a shabby place to be abducted."

As John walked away, Maggie turned around and was immediately drawn to a colorful, massive abstract painting prominently hung in the lobby. Walking towards it she thought, *this looks like a Bob Ichter.* She scrutinized every inch of the oversize canvas, admiring his use of intense competing colors.

She had no idea that John had returned and was standing behind her. He startled her when he said, "The hotel commissioned Bob Ichter to do this; it's titled, *Seas of Europa*."

Maggie turned to him and said, "I'm impressed my abductor knows so much about art."

"Let's discuss this over cocktails. I've booked two rooms on the Club Level."

She preferred a room on the first floor. Still, she stepped inside the dark paneled elevator. The brass doors closed; John pushed the twenty-fourth-floor button. Moving in next to him, she grasped his hand like a frightened child. Trying not to sound nervous, she asked, "How long will it take us to get to our floor?"

"Hopefully fast, I've already been far too patient today." The elevator made a *bing* sound, and Maggie's anxiety vanished as the door slid opened.

John handed her a keycard to room 2421. "Why don't we freshen up, and I'll order some champagne. Come to my room 2423, next door, around six-thirty."

Maggie sank down on the king size bed pondering her current situation. *It's not like it's the first time I've had a one-night stand.* On New Year's Eve her close friend, Sharon, convinced her it was time to venture into the dating world once again. Now, only five days later, Maggie had checked into a hotel with a complete stranger. She decided it would be wise to text Sharon and let her know about her unexpected change of plans for the night and where she was staying.

Fortunately, she had packed everything in a carry-on bag, including her Christmas present from Sharon, a new Jimmyjane waterproof cordless vibrator. She placed it on the marble ledge of the tub. As she emptied the hotel's Asprey shower gel under the warm running water, a divine scent of citrus ginger engulfed the room.

Underneath the frothy suds, she imagined resting in the shallow end of the ocean with the waves breaking against her. When she was just a precocious child, she would often do this on the beach after discovering what a tingling sensation it would cause to her private parts. Bessie, the family housekeeper, would ask her why she had so much sand in the bottom of her swimsuit and tell her to wash off good down there. Young Maggie learned how sensual the roughness of the washcloth could be. Now she had the luxury of a vibrator to arouse her. As she eased it in and out, her idle hand rubbed her wet erect nipples in perfect sync. She envisioned Chris making love to her on a secluded beach. Caught up in her fantasy, she moved the vibrator faster while pulling and squeezing her nipples until she released herself into her imaginary ocean.

Having lost track of time, she quickly changed into her new red dress and her favorite black stilettos that raised her five-foot-six-inch height four inches taller. Viewing herself in the bathroom mirror, she admired the sexy backless design. She cringed when she saw her visible panty line; she removed her panties. Her nipples showed their excitement through the clingy fabric; pinching them made them more noticeable. She scrutinized her face in the mirror and touched up her makeup.

Taking a deep inhale, she knocked on room 2423. John opened it wearing a towel tied around his waist, showing off his toned six-pack abs. Caught off-guard, she said, "I guess I'm overdressed. Do you have an extra towel I can wear?"

John smiled back. "Please come in. You look ravishing."

Inside the suite's living area, his hand slid underneath her dress stopping at the top of her hipbone. He detected her lack of underwear. "You're quite a tease."

Maggie smelled the now familiar citrus and ginger spice he had used in the shower. She wanted to reach underneath the towel and exchange greetings, but he moved away from her.

"I just got out of the shower. I was tied up on the phone, had to cancel a dinner meeting for tonight. Would you like some champagne while I finish getting dressed?"

"Champagne sounds wonderful." As she admired the spacious living room area, which included a library, wet bar, and formal dining area, she commented, "What a magnificent suite."

After pouring her champagne, he headed to the bedroom. At the doorway he turned to Maggie, "Is your room okay?"

"Oh, yes. I rank this in the top ten places to be abducted."

"Our rooms adjoin. Go unlock your door; I've unlocked mine."

Maggie waited on the sectional sofa for his return. Without hesitation, she had done what he had ask of her. She took several sips of the champagne, hoping it would lessen her uneasiness. John walked into the living area running his fingers through his damp, wavy hair. He was dressed in medium-rise, straight-cut jeans, a light blue cashmere sweater that matched his eyes, and loafers without socks. Maggie's eyes followed him as he walked to the expanse of windows and opened the drapes revealing a magical light display coming from the Centennial Olympic Park.

He turned and stared at Maggie as if he knew a dark hidden secret about her. "I'm flattered that you feel attracted to me."

Maggie nervously took a sip of champagne. "I guess this dress gives me away?"

As he walked over to get his champagne, he said, "I detected it earlier in the airport by observing your body language. You're good at getting men to notice you."

"You'd already undressed me with your eyes in the boarding area."

17

"You're sexy. Obviously, you know that already."

Flustered, Maggie replied, "Perhaps…this was not a good idea…me coming here with you."

"You knew the risk. Now stand up and do as I say."

"Excuse me?"

"You heard what I said. I don't like to repeat myself."

"And what if I don't?"

"Let me remedy the problem of your being overdressed."

She stood up next to him. His hand traveled up the slit of her dress again, veering to her crotch. This was the first time in almost two years she'd allowed a man to touch her, she started swaying as his skilled hand stroked her. Unconsciously she was biting her lip, anticipating what would follow.

"Turn around."

Maggie quivered as he ran his finger down her naked spine. He pulled the straps off her shoulders allowing the dress to drop to the floor. She stepped over it in her stilettos and turned slightly towards him.

He told her, "Don't."

He held her firmly and leaned against her backside. His bulging cock inside his jeans rubbed against her. She began shuddering as his large hands cupped her ample breasts and squeezed her delicate nipples.

The torment he inflicted on her nipples caused a burning sensation in her crotch; she moaned at the sweet pain. He lowered his hands and pulled her legs slightly apart sliding his index finger inside her. He whispered into her ear, "You're juicy like a ripe peach. Turn around and unfasten my jeans."

Maggie slipped her hand underneath his jeans, grasping him. He abruptly pulled her hand away.

"What's wrong?"

In a perplexed tone, he said, "I can see you don't like being told what to do."

"It depends on what it is."

"Let me give you the benefit of the doubt this time; unzip my jeans."

He had already kicked off his loafers. Even in her four-inch stilettos, he towered over her. She instinctively kneeled in front of him, took possession of his bulging zipper and started moving her hungry mouth towards his wonderful treasure. Within an inch of her target, he grabbed her hair and pulled her back up.

For a minute, Maggie stared into his eyes, in a hypnotic trance as he finished removing his jeans and took off his sweater. Grabbing her hand, he led her to the bedroom. The drapes were fully open and the millions of lights illuminating the skyline cast a sensual glow inside the dark room. He walked over to the bedside table and turned on a brass reading lamp.

"Take your shoes off and sit down over here."

Hearing an authoritative tone in his voice, Maggie dared not obey.

"Now lean back."

He moved the reading lamp closer to the bed and adjusted the light so it illuminated between her loins. He pulled her legs wide apart visually inspecting every inch of her before he probed inside her. Her whole body was electrified. Every nerve ending fired off as he explored her.

"By chance, did you bring a vibrator with you?"

"Why would you ask such a personal question?"

"Get it, and bring that scarf you wore earlier."

A few minutes later, she returned with her sex toy storage bag. There was an ice bucket on the bedside table and a white towel spread out on the bed.

John said, "Let me see what you have."

She unlocked the bag and handed it to him.

19

As he examined her toys, he said, "You took these on the airplane with you? Aren't you afraid you might get stopped?"

"I did one time. I smiled at the security agent and told him how I couldn't travel without them. He winked at me and let me go right through."

John had picked up her favorite vibrator. "Do you use this one often?"

"When I've had a stressful day--better than eating a pint of Ben & Jerry's ice cream."

"Did you have a stressful day today? I see there are drops of water on it."

"It works well in the bathtub."

"I hope you didn't run down the battery."

"It stays charged for quite a while."

"Show me how you like to use these?"

"Demonstrate?"

"Just imagine you're in the bedroom next door and don't have any Ben & Jerry's ice cream. I want to see what turns you on."

Oddly, he had made her feel totally uninhibited. She reclined on the bed, propping herself up on two pillows. He watched in erotic pleasure as she moaned for him to take her please before she climaxed. He commanded, "Keep your vibrator in and sit up."

Taking her scarf, he covered her eyes, tying the silk gently from behind. In her blinded state, she was vulnerable and powerless, unable to anticipate what would happen next. She barely knew this man, which aroused her further.

"Now grasp your hands behind your neck and imagine I've tied you up."

Enmeshed in wild fantasy, this total stranger made her his submissive. While in her professional life Maggie exercised control, here in this stranger's bed, it felt so natural to allow someone else to possess her, to take control of her will and soul, to strip her inhibitions, and force her to yearn for pain and ecstasy.

The clinking of ice in the bucket startled her. The sharp coldness numbed her nipple. He fervently sucked until the numbness disappeared. To her dismay, everything stopped, and she lay captive wondering what would happen next.

The ice clinked again, and her left nipple became victimized.

"Open your mouth."

She squirmed with anticipation as he pressed an ice cube against her throat, slowly running down the center of her body, until it rested on her naval. He slowly pressed the cube down her belly, removed the vibrator, and replaced the freezing ice deep inside her.

"Get back on your knees."

He helped her off the bed. She doubted that she would be able to accommodate his massive cock. The tip brushed across her lips. She eagerly swallowed him, careful not to gag.

John directed her, "Use your hand up and down and touch my balls."

Maggie was an expert at following these types of directions.

"Now stop and get on your hands and knees."

Never before had she experienced the type of fullness, as he pressed his cock inside her. Holding her hips, he drove deeper, inflicting the pleasurable pain Maggie so desired.

"I want you to get on top. Let me take your blindfold off."

He allowed Maggie to control their sexual exchange, her rhythm at first sultry and slow. He sat up while she faced him; her legs wrapped around his torso, enabling him to penetrate deeper. Covered in a sea of sweat, they pounded into one another. Maggie was like an animal clawing at his back each time he hit her sweet spot.

Their bodies were exhausted after they reached crescendo. John broke their silence, "Let's get some dinner downstairs."

"Would you mind if we order room service; I'd rather not get dressed again?"

Wearing a Ritz Carlton bathrobe, Maggie stretched out on the chaise end of the sectional sofa to watch The Weather Channel. John sat down next to her, pouring champagne into her glass.

"I'm glad you suggested we order room service."

"John, are you purposely avoiding answering me about whether you're married?"

"No, not at all. I've just had a bad track record, been divorced three times."

"How about any children?"

"Twins, Annie and Jack, from my second marriage."

"How old are they?"

"Twelve."

"Do you see them often?"

"Unfortunately, no; they're at Le Rosey, in Rolle, Switzerland. I see them a week during the holidays and then half their summer vacation. I just spent a week with them in Maui during Christmas. I'll next see them during their summer vacation in July. We're taking a road trip to several of the National Parks and renting a house in Whitefish, Montana."

"Who decided to send them to boarding school?"

"Not me, I assure you. Their mother went to the same boarding school; she insisted they go there."

"I was sent away to the same boarding school that my mother and grandmother attended. I'm planning on breaking this family tradition. I want to enjoy my kids as long as I can. Excuse me while I freshen up."

Maggie returned dressed in a matching red silk robe and gown, a Christmas present from her business partner and former lover, Matthew. Even after their amicable breakup, Matthew still enjoyed buying her sexy lingerie.

John was talking on his cell phone; she kneeled down and parted his robe. Putting the crown of his cock in her mouth, she encircled its tip with her tongue while slowly massaging his sensitive perineum.

"Sorry, I can't make our appointment tomorrow. I will see you Tuesday. Ahh…I have to take another call."

As he hung up his phone, Maggie said, "Got your attention. Have you ever wanted someone to sexually dominate you?"

"Why, are you interested?"

"Because you seem to be the type who's always in control, even in your personal life."

"Come lie down with me on the sofa."

John pulled her into his strong arms. "Sometimes I fantasize about meeting an attractive woman like you at a hotel bar. I'm invited to her room where we have incredible sex together and fall asleep. During the early morning hours, I wake up and find my hands and feet tied to the bedposts. The woman is wearing a strapless black lace bustier with garters fastened to black fishnet hose. Her low-cut bustier exposes her nipples. A riding crop lies next to me. She's straddled over me, facing away, sucking on my cock. I'm her prisoner, under her complete control."

"Are you sure that's not a real story?"

"Wish it was."

Waking up to the smell of coffee, Maggie grabbed her robe and joined John in the living area.

John said, "I've some disappointing news. We have two first class seats on the ten o'clock morning flight. What are your plans while you're in New York?"

"What do you have in mind?"

"Stay with me."

CHAPTER THREE

NEW YORK

As they rode the limo to John's New York condo, he squeezed Maggie's hand and said, "I know my place isn't convenient to your gallery, but I look forward to spending more time with you."

"Are you sure? We have a saying in the South that guests, like fish, begin to smell after three days."

"Do you know where that phrase originated?"

"Sorry, I was never good at trivial pursuit."

"Ben Franklin. Speaking of fish, where would you like to have dinner tonight?"

Maggie hesitated, "I, I already have dinner plans." John let go of her hand and was silent. Feeling guilty, she added, "With my business partner."

Maggie suspected he was not pleased with her plans. She gave him a reassuring smile. "We need to catch up on business."

John remained silent, which magnified Maggie's anxiety.

She cleared her throat and continued, "Except for tonight, I'm free until Friday night. We're having an artist reception. I would love for you to come."

"I'll check my schedule." John left hand squeezed Maggie's right thigh. Don't make any additional evening plans."

Maggie dug her long fingernails into the top of John's hand. "So you're putting conditions on me staying here?"

"Save your claws for later, my back needs scratching. Let's just say I want to maximize the time we spend together."

It was after 4 p.m. when they arrived at John's condo building at 15 Broad Street. In the lobby, John pointed out the elaborate Louis XV crystal chandelier. "This chandelier was originally in the lobby of the adjoining building that once housed JP Morgan's offices."

"It's quite beautiful. Which floor are we heading to?"

"Thirty-nine."

Maggie took a deep breath and said, "Oh, my."

"What's wrong? Are you afraid of heights?"

"While I've learned to tolerate airplanes, elevators are different. I take the stairs whenever possible."

"I sensed that when you squeezed my hand on takeoff and landing."

Inside the elevator, John pressed her against the wall and firmly kissed her. Like magic, Maggie's fear diminished.

As John opened his entry door, Maggie was speechless as she saw the floor to ceiling bank of windows, which framed a birds-eye view of the Empire State Building.

"I love your view… and all the windows…although I don't dare stand next to them. Do you come here often?"

"I got tired of staying in hotels. A former law partner of mine owned it. It was about to go into foreclosure. I ended up bailing Rick out. Let me show you around."

Surprising to Maggie, the master bedroom had a traditionally styled, mahogany, four-poster bed while the rest of the décor was more contemporary. As in the living room, the ceiling was vaulted, and there were two large windows with spectacular city views.

"Nice bathroom. You have a lot of mirrors. I bet your cleaning person has to use a whole Windex bottle in here."

She followed John into the second bedroom, which was small, but efficient, just enough room for two twin beds and a long dresser. Its marble bathroom had a tub-shower combo.

John asked, "When do you have to meet your business partner?"

"Seven-thirty at Café Boulud."

"That's at The Surrey. You'll need to leave here around seven. How about unpacking? You can use the dresser and closet in the guest room. I'll get us some wine."

Maggie finished unpacking and put on her red silk robe. She met John in the kitchen where he had poured their wine. Barefoot and wearing only his sweatpants, he slipped his hands underneath her robe, fondling her breasts.

"I've been horny all day; I wanted to join the mile high club."

"Why didn't you? That blonde flight attendant had the *hots* for you."

"I've a thing for redheads." As he took her hand and positioned it on his bulging crotch, he said, "I can sense you want this. Let's go into the bedroom so I can give you an appetizer before you go out."

Within minutes, both were satiated. The last thing Maggie wanted to do was to get up and meet Matthew for dinner. She rushed through her shower, put on the red dress she had worn briefly the previous night, and found John on the sofa working on his laptop. He gestured for her to come over.

"You're wearing this dress to a business dinner? Sure it's not a date?"

"We have a platonic relationship."

"A platonic relationship, have you ever had sex with him?"

"The relationship ended several years ago."

"We'll discuss this later; it's almost time for you to go."

"I need to get my coat."

27

"I hung it in the foyer closet. I'll get it."

As he helped her with her coat, he said, "Maybe you need to keep your coat on tonight and keep your scarf on as well. By the way, I've reviewed the restaurant's menu online, and I suggest that you don't overindulge. I've got plans for us later tonight. Give me your cell number and keep your phone on in case I need to contact you. A taxi will be here in five minutes. You shouldn't have any problems getting a return taxi at the hotel. I've written my address and my cell number on the back of my business card."

Maggie put his card into her purse. "Here's my business card; text to the 251 area code number."

"Come here."

Maggie walked over to John. He pulled her in and kissed her. "Umm. I like this kissing part. Sure you can't cancel your date tonight?"

"That would be rude. It's not a date."

He gazed into her bewitching eyes. "Keep your phone near."

"May I ask you a favor? I hate to walk down thirty-nine floors in these heels. Would you ride the elevator down with me?"

"Only if you'll let me kiss you all the way down. Why don't you take your vibrator along for your ride up tonight? That will hopefully distract you. I think we need a name for it."

She smiled. "How about 'Buzz'?"

It had been over three months since she had seen Matthew. He was the type of guy who stood out in a crowd, definitely a looker, with his Italian heritage. His deceased father was from Northern Italy, over six feet tall, blond hair, and blue eyes while his mother was from Sicily, barely five feet tall, dark brown hair, and brown eyes. He was the perfect blend of his Italian parents, tall like his father but brown hair and eyes like his mother. Matthew had been a professional model for five years before he worked at his first gallery. It hadn't surprised Maggie when she found out that he was bi-sexual. He admitted it to her the first night they had sex. He told her that he discovered his unconventional sexual appetite when he met Paul, another professional model.

Matthew was waiting for her at their usual table. They hugged and kissed each other.

"Doll, you look stunning in that dress."

"Found it on the etsy website. It was on sale."

"Have you ever paid full price for anything?"

"When it comes to relationships, I have. Speaking of which, Chris has contacted me again. He sent me a book he wrote."

"Have you read it?"

"Not yet. He wants me to contact him."

Maggie glanced at her phone and saw a text message. When Matthew excused himself, she took the opportunity to read it.

"Too much rich French food for what I've planned tonight. Order this:
Winter Squash Soup
Vietnamese Seafood Salad
Fresh Citrus Meyer Lemon, Tarragon, Mimosa Sorbet
And limit your alcohol to two glasses."

Maggie texted back:

"I don't want the Vietnamese Seafood Salad."

"Then order the Wild Alaskan King Salmon."

After finishing the first course, Maggie saw another text from John.

"Go to the ladies room and call me."

"It's good that you followed my directions. I put Buzz into your purse. Climax before returning to dinner. Imagine I'm taking you from behind. That's my plan for you tonight."

After Maggie composed herself, she returned to the table.

29

Matthew asked, "Why can't you get inspired to paint again? Your paintings brought top dollar at the gallery."

"I've told you this before. I have no desire right now."

"You mean you have to be getting laid, like you did when you lived with Sean."

"Please--don't bring him up."

"My cousin is a narcissistic sociopath. Doll, I'm sorry. I still get mad about how he treated you."

"I'm over him."

"Are you in a new relationship? You have a special glow, like you did when we were having our tête-à-tête."

"I've changed my workout routine."

"Hopefully, you'll once again allow me your pleasures."

"After our tête-à-tête, as you like to call it, we made a pact not to let our personal desires influence our business goals."

Matthew sighed, "If we ever sell the gallery, will you reconsider?"

"It's getting late. I need to leave."

"I'm sure you're tired; let me escort you to your room."

"I'm not staying here."

Matthew looked surprised. "And why not?"

"Let's get a taxi, and I'll fill you in."

While riding in the taxi, Matthew placed his hand on Maggie's thigh and continued his inquisition. "So, you met Mr. Strange yesterday at the Atlanta airport...he invited you to his private layover party at the downtown Ritz, and *now* you'll be staying with him in his New York love nest the rest of this week?"

"Do you think I'm crazy?"

"I just think you're horny. Does he have a nice package?"

"I've claimed it already."

Maggie remembered she needed to text John.
"I'll be at your condo soon."
"The door will be unlocked."
"Wouldn't you like to meet me downstairs?"
John didn't answer.

Matthew said, "If you start painting again, we can have a special exhibit this summer. I want your work back in the gallery, even if it means you being screwed by Mr. Strange."

"Matthew, you sound like my pimp; I just met this guy. It's only my second night seeing him. I'm not in a relationship."

Sedated from the wine and champagne, at least two more glasses than John had allotted her, Maggie took the elevator to the thirty-ninth floor. As she entered the room, John shut down his laptop and said, "Welcome back."

Not wanting to get busted, Maggie concentrated on walking a straight line to the kitchen table where John sat. He removed her outer coat.

"I'll pour us some cognac while you get more comfortable."

"You wouldn't have a robe I could borrow?"

"I have one hanging on the door hook in my bathroom."

Maggie returned wearing John's flannel robe. It smelled woodsy and musky like his aftershave. She recognized the scent as Guess Seductive, the same aftershave Matthew wore.

"That looks much nicer on you than me. Let's sit down on the sofa. How was your dinner?"

"Nice."

"How is Matthew doing?"

Maggie choked as she replied, "I don't recall telling you his name; how did you know?"

31

"Google also told me you're an artist and had an exhibit in 2010. I'm impressed with the style of your work, extremely erotic."

Maggie crossed her arms in front. "What else did you find out?"

"I like how you sign your paintings, Maggie O'. An art critic called you, the steel magnolia shocking the art world."

"You've been busy tonight."

"It's amazing what you can find out. Tell me about the relationship you were in when you painted then?"

"You couldn't find that out?

"Just that you used his nude photographs of you to paint from."

"He betrayed me."

"Was he married?"

A master at holding back her tears, Maggie turned away and gazed out the window. The stabbing pain was back. John refilled her glass. After taking a long sip, she turned back to him and said, "They were separated. He hid from me that he had a son."

John shook his head, "He didn't tell you that detail?"

"No, and who knows what else he didn't tell me. I couldn't trust him anymore."

"How did you meet him?"

Maggie was certain that John had figured out she'd broken the two-drink rule and now with this truth drug "Hennessy XO", her inhibitions had vanished.

John slid his arm behind Maggie's neck and shoulders. "You don't have to explain."

"I met him when I lived in Atlanta. He was on a business trip, a photojournalist with National Geographic. Eleven months later he convinced me to resign my job and live with him in Chicago. We both became obsessed with one another. He would take these lascivious photos of me. I painted the erotic nymph series from his photos."

"You are an extremely talented artist; why did you stop painting?"

"When I stopped seeing him, I lost the passion. The creative fire within me was extinguished."

"You just need the right inspiration to get going again."

"Perhaps. Matthew keeps bugging me to start painting again. Tonight he offered to do a show for me this summer."

John poured them both more cognac, then settled his hand on Maggie's knee. She rested her head against his shoulder. "Tell me about your relationship with Matthew and how you formed this business alliance?"

"He's Sean's first cousin. They grew up together in an Italian Chicago neighborhood. Matthew came to visit us one weekend. He was captivated by the three nymph paintings and asked me to do an exclusive exhibit at the New York gallery he managed. At the pre-party for my opening exhibit, Matthew asked me if I'd ever met Sean's son. I was totally shocked.

"Fast forward six months later—I'm healing my wounds by sleeping with Matthew and forming a new business plan for a unique kind of art gallery. That's when The Launch was born."

"Have you seen Sean since you broke up with him?"

"Fortunately, I'm never in our gallery when he comes in. Matthew told me he divorced his wife."

"You need to relax. You're way too tense. Let's go to the bedroom. I'll give you a backrub."

John had staged his bedroom for her return. His signature Burberry ties were fastened to the bedposts. Maggie recognized Kenny G's *Songbird* playing in the background. Disrobed, she faced down on the towel he had placed on the bed. John removed his sweat pants and t-shirt and straddled her, massaging sweet almond oil on her stiff neck.

John moved down her tense spine. As he proceeded further south, she moaned, "You're arousing me."

"All in good time. Relax for now."

He moved on to her legs, kneading each muscle group from her thighs all the way down to her feet.

"Now turn over."

She dreaded turning over. During sex you aren't as visually focused on the person's anatomy as you are during a massage. She felt as though she were on a petri dish underneath a microscope.

John massaged the tops of her feet and between her toes. His touch warmed her body. He kneaded her calves and then her thighs. The further he moved upward, the more aroused she became.

"Let's take a hot shower so I can wash this oil off you."

When Maggie saw the shower she said, "You could fit a banquet table in here."

"It actually was a third bedroom."

Maggie watched as he adjusted the various levels of showerheads. Satisfied, he turned to her, "Ladies first."

After he had lathered her hair and body, he moved her so that the water hit her at all angles. She said, "This reminds me of the water sprinkler fights we had as kids."

"I need to make a few adjustments. Turn around and face this wall. This one needs to be lower and these two need to come up a bit higher. There that's perfect." The water was pelting both her nipples. "How does that feel?"

"Like Chinese erotic water torture. Did you design this shower?"

"My buddy had it designed. Now sit on the bench and lean back, relax, and enjoy the water torture. I need to send a text to a colleague."

Maggie sat down next to John at the kitchen table. John handed her a bottle of water and said, "I've an interesting proposition for you. I want you to see if you can dominate me."

"You don't like to be dominated."

"That's the point. You need to figure out how you can change that. I gave you a clue last night when I told you my fantasy. Tomorrow I'll let you know the hotel where we'll meet in the bar. Go shopping for something appropriate to wear and a riding crop, unless you brought one with you."

Maggie grinned, "They wouldn't let me take my riding crop through security."

CHAPTER FOUR

THE FAIRY GODFATHER

Maggie sent an emergency alert. "I need your guidance. Will you go shopping with me?"

"I'll get Connie to cover for us. We can leave right after our appointment with Richard Marks, the blind sculptor I told you about. See you at ten."

After the appointment, Matthew said, "I ordered us a quick lunch from the deli next door."

"Hope you got me that pastrami sandwich I love."

"I ordered you a Greek salad; you don't want to be bloated tonight."

"You're as controlling as someone else I know."

"Admit it; you like that quality in men. This should be fun, kind of like going on a scavenger hunt. I've several stores in mind. We'll start at Babeland here in SoHo."

"I found this riding crop. I like how the handle is also a glass dildo. You'll need these too."

Maggie grabbed the box and read it. "How clever, Bondage in a Box."

"Just in case you have to anchor to the legs of the bed. Most hotel beds only have a headboard."

"You sound like you've done this before."

"I had a short affair with a guy who was really into BDSM. His apartment was like a torture chamber."

"Which role did you play?"

"We switched."

"Well, now I know who to consult."

"Don't play innocent with me; I know well your masochist needs. You're the most uninhibited female I've ever known. That's why your erotic paintings are amazing."

"Let me go ahead and pay for this."

"Now we need to get you some sexy lingerie. You remember La Petite Coquette, where I like to buy your lingerie; let's go there next."

As they sat in the backseat of the taxi, Matthew tapped Maggie's thigh with the riding crop. "Can I borrow this from you sometime?"

"Get your own."

Matthew found a black sheer dotted tulle bustier. "This should fit you. It has garters so you don't have to wear a garter belt. Do you like it?"

"I better try it on; be back in a minute."

"I want to go in with you."

"Wait outside."

After Maggie put it on over her nude thong, she invited him in.

"My, my, my. If this outfit doesn't turn him on, he should be castrated. Turn around and let me see the back--provocative." He squeezed her ass and said, "I miss your cute little booty. A man's booty isn't nearly as attractive as a woman's. Remember that time we got caught in the dressing room. I'm getting a hard-on just thinking about it."

Matthew moved his hand to her crotch sliding it underneath her thong.

Maggie moved his hand away. "Stop that and get out of here."

37

"You need something special to wear underneath. I'll start looking while you get dressed."

Now in street clothes, she found Matthew talking to a young blonde sales clerk. He held a black lace thong with two strands of pearls strategically placed to rub against the crotch. Maggie said, "That's an unusual way to wear pearls."

Matthew turned back to the clerk, "Lilly, tell her about these."

"That's one of our best-selling thongs. It's called Bracli taken from two Spanish words, Braga which means underwear, and I'm sure you can guess what the c-l-i means."

Matthew blurted out, "Clitoris, how clever. We'll take one in red and one in black. I see they make a body suit. Lilly, we'll take one in black."

Matthew handed Lilly his credit card.

Maggie pulled him aside. "What are you doing? You can't buy these for me?"

"Why not? Consider it a late birthday present. I'll have the gratification of knowing that I still can bring some sexual excitement in your life when you wear these."

"Honestly, what am I going to do with you?"

"We've got one more stop. Let's get on our way. Unless you want to have a quickie in the dressing room."

Matthew told the cabbie, "Kiki de Montparnasse, 79 Greene Street in Lower Manhattan."

"I'm excited. I've read about this store."

Matthew said, "They cater to affluent customers, great selection of upscale sex toys and high-end lingerie."

Maggie squeezed Matthew's hand. "I can't thank you enough for helping me today."

Dazzled by the store, Maggie had not noticed that John had sent a text message.

"Hotel Elysée, 60 East 54th Street. Be at The Monkey Bar at 7:30. I booked it under your name. In a boring meeting now; I'll see you in less than four hours."

Matthew returned to her. "We have to hurry. I found you this black jersey dress to try on. They have taken it to the dressing room. Have you heard back from Mr. Stranger where you rendezvous with him tonight?"

Maggie retrieved her phone from her purse. *"Hotel Elysée."*

"Rocambolesco."

Maggie loved how the racer backed dress formed to her hourglass body and showed off her cleavage, shoulders, and arms. The hem hit two inches above her knee, and the leather choker collar gave it an edgy dominatrix flare. "Do you think it's too daring?"

"That looks hotter on you than I imagined. You're done shopping; let's get out of here."

"Here's my phone. I want you to take a picture of me so I can get John's approval."

"Do you realize you just said you want to get his approval? You desperately want to please this guy. Wait, you need to have a prop. Hold the riding crop in your hand. Look like a dominatrix. Perfect. Now get dressed; we need to get out of here."

Maggie walked over to Matthew. "I'm going to kill you; this dress costs over three grand. Find me something cheaper."

"It's an investment you won't regret."

"What's in the Kiki bag?"

"A few items you might need. I'll show them to you later."

Maggie noticed a second text from John.

"I already have a hard on seeing the photo you just sent. Love the dress. However, I need to stay focused on this meeting instead of our plans for tonight."

"Sorry to have disrupted your meeting. Sounds like you need to turn your phone off."

Matthew said, "Let's hurry; we need to get you checked into your hotel."

"You don't have to come with me."

"Are you kidding? I wouldn't miss it. I feel like your fairy godfather."

Maggie and Matthew took a cab to John's condo to pick up Maggie's suitcase, then headed over to the hotel.

The taxi driver, Josh, a retired English teacher, gave them a brief history lesson. "Built in the 1920's, the Hotel Elysée is a famous New York Landmark. Tennessee Williams lived his last fifteen years in what is now called the Sunset Suite. In fact, he wrote all of his later plays in this suite. In 1983, he was found dead in his room."

When Maggie saw the Hotel Elysée red awning, she felt like Cinderella arriving at the palace. "I remember meeting Susan and Don for drinks at The Monkey Bar."

"I'm surprised you remember that night. You were mourning your breakup with Sean."

Maggie lowered her voice to a whisper, "And that was the night you took advantage of me."

Matthew whispered back, "You practically raped me, if you'll recall."

Matthew included thirty percent gratuity when he paid Josh, while a bellman loaded his cart with the suitcase and all the shopping items from the cab.

The hotel's Art Deco style lobby enchanted Maggie. It reminded her of an European luxury hotel with its intricate patterned marble floors--including a large compass star medallion, glittering crystal chandelier, gold brocade wallpaper, and lavish furnishings.

At the front desk, a pleasant young man said to her, "A gentleman was here earlier and already checked you in. You're in the Horowitz Suite; Joe will take you there. On the second floor, is our Club Room. We have a wine and cheese reception from five to eight."

Joe said, "Let's take the lift to your suite on the twelfth floor."

As they rode up, Joe said, "You're staying in one of our three Presidential Suites. Virtuoso pianist, Vladimir Horowitz, took up temporary residence at the hotel during the 1970's. He even had a Steinway baby grand moved into his suite. When he later checked out, he told the hotel manager to keep it."

The suite's living–dining area had a stately but peaceful ambiance with its coffered ceiling and paneled walls. Counting the six dining room chairs, the room could comfortably seat eighteen. The rectangular formal dining table anchored one side of the room, and the infamous Horowitz Steinway piano anchored the other side. In the center, twin damask covered loveseats flanked the Neoclassical style fireplace. On the opposing windowed exterior wall, a flat panel LCD television perched on top of an inlaid wooden French chest. In addition, the room easily accommodated a writing desk and several occasional chairs. Hidden on the other side of the fireplace wall was a small kitchenette.

Maggie could picture Horowitz seeking refuge here. She admired the original oil paintings displayed that she guessed were from the nineteenth century. She and Matthew followed Joe back to the bedroom. The bedroom area was elegant, with a canopied bed and a large mirrored armoire next to the bed. Matthew walked over to the bed and pulled up the dust ruffle. He said, "Good thing I got that rope. I have to cut it and tie it to the legs of the bed. I'm glad I brought my pocket knife."

Joe overheard Matthew. He chuckled to himself and said, "I think you'll both find our mattresses are comfortable. This door goes out to a terrace overlooking 54th Street. Would you like me to get you some ice?"

Matthew grabbed Maggie by the waist, snuggled her up to his hip and said, "Yes, please. You can't imagine how steamy it will get in here later tonight."

Maggie played along with his charade. "I'm hungry, sweetie. That salad didn't fill me up. If you expect any action tonight, then let's go get some wine and a snack."

As she tipped Joe, she said, "We may be gone when you return."

Downstairs in the Club Room, Maggie said, "I'm nervous. I need a glass of Prosecco."

Matthew filled a plate with cheese, crackers, and fruit. "Why don't we sit down on that white sofa next to the window?"

Maggie raised her champagne flute, "To my dearest fairy godfather, thank you for helping me today."

Their glasses clinked as they both said, "Cheers!"

"Do you know that until these last two days with Mr. Strange, I've not had sex with anyone in almost two years."

"I find that hard to believe. You could've always slept with me again."

"After you and I broke up, I had a string of one-night stands. Also several blind dates Mary set me up with. I finally gave up on finding love again."

"I had no idea you were going through such a morose phase in your life. With your ravenous sexual appetite, it must have been difficult."

"Fortunately, I found mechanical ways to relieve myself, which was great. I didn't have to worry about how I looked or wonder if anyone was cheating on me." Maggie looked down at her phone and said, "It's already six."

"I think it's time for me to disappear. I must warn you, if you haven't dominated Prince Charming by midnight, you may lose him forever."

"Where are my glass slippers?"

"Glass slippers are obsolete. Besides the only anatomy he wants to fit into is your Vajayjay. You need to get ready." Matthew noticed Maggie biting her lip. "Are you okay?"

"I'm about to have a meltdown. Please don't go. I need your help."

"Let's go back to the room."

"Doll, while you shower, I'll work on the bed restraints."

Maggie adjusted the water temperature. She slid Buzz in and out while allowing the full force of the shower spray to pelt her upper body. After a needed climax, she lathered up her legs to shave.

Maggie screamed, "Ouch. I can't believe it; I nicked myself."

He entered the bathroom. "Honestly, I can't leave you alone for one second. Do I need to call an ambulance?"

Matthew shook his head in disbelief as he picked up Buzz and placed it on the bathtub's ledge. "Talk about multi-tasking, perhaps you wouldn't cut yourself if you didn't use your vibrator at the same time. I will help you shave your legs and any other area you need shaved."

"Thanks, but I just had a Brazilian wax job."

After she finished bathing, Matthew said, "You know how much men like their prostate massaged, you need to shorten your nails."

"But I just got this deluxe manicure."

"Get your priorities straight. Here are your nail scissors. Let me show you how short."

After he had shortened her pointer fingernail, Maggie protested, "Hey that's short."

"Complain about that when he is enjoying his P-spot massage."

After de-clawing herself, she asked, "How should I wear my hair, up or down?"

"In a loose bun, to show off the back of your dress."

Matthew had her new outfit displayed on the bed. He said, "I suggest you put on the red pearl thong."

Maggie giggled like a preteen as she started walking in her new thong.

"Just remember who gave them to you whenever you wear them."

"They deserve a Good Housekeeping Award. Can you help me put on my dress? I'm nervous about tonight."

"You have a script already of what he wants. How often does that happen? Put this blindfold on. I want you to be surprised. Since there's no zipper, I'll undo the choke collar and pull it over your head… Sit on the edge of the bed, while I help you with your shoes…now, walk over to the mirror with me."

In front of the large mirrored armoire, Matthew removed her blindfold.

"I feel so empowered in this dress."

"There are condoms, breath mints, lubes, and some votive candles on the bedside table. Also some candles in the bathroom. Most important, remember to use the silicone lubricate when you massage his P-spot."

"You've thought of everything. Thank you."

"It's time for Cinderella to make her appearance. I want a full report tomorrow. I'll ride down with you."

CHAPTER FIVE

CINDERELLA'S FANTASY

The risqué nature of her dress made her feel self-conscious as she chose a seat at the bar. The bartender brought a glass of ice water and said, "Would you like to look at our drink menu? You might want to try one of our Monkey Bar Cocktails."

Maggie noticed his nametag. "I'll have the house Pinot Noir."

Barry returned with the wine. "Where are you from? I detect a Southern accent."

"Gulf Shores, Alabama."

"My relatives live near there in Mobile. I visited them several years ago during Mardi Gras."

"You don't have a Northern accent; where are you from?"

"Cleveland."

Maggie eyed John coming into the bar and watched him sit down at a nearby table. A busty waitress wasted no time taking his drink order. Maggie watched as John spoke to her. The waitress came over to the bar and started talking with Barry. After a few minutes, Barry came to Maggie and said, "The gentleman over there would like you to join him at his table."

"Would you mind asking him to be so kind and personally introduce himself to me first?"

A few minutes later, John came over to the bar and said, "Touché. You're good at this."

Maggie ignored the familiarity of his comment and sent a glacier remark back his way. "I'm sorry, have we met before?"

45

After exchanging their names, John said, "An attractive woman like you shouldn't be alone; would you care for some company?"

"How presumptuous you are, Mr. Kramer. Actually I was about to return to my suite."

"How about joining me later for dinner?"

Maggie stood up and directly faced John. "Would you like having some champagne in my suite while I consider your invitation?"

The elevator was crowded; a group was headed to the eleventh floor. John whispered in Maggie's ear, "They'll be getting off first. Let's move to the back."

Wrapping his arms around her, he pulled her in tightly. The hardness of his crotch vanished her fear of heights. John continued to hold and press against her as the group exited the elevator. The door opened on the next floor, and he released her.

Maggie unlocked the suite's door, "Please come in and have a seat, or would you prefer leaning against the wall instead?"

"What other options do you have in mind?"

"Please excuse me for a moment; help yourself to some champagne."

Maggie returned noticing that John's suit jacket and his red Burberry tie were hanging on the back of a dining chair. Handing her a glass, he said, "Do you often invite strangers up to your hotel room?"

Maggie placed her glass on the dining table and walked backwards several steps until she was an inch away from the damask paneled wall, "Shall we ride up and down in the elevator again?"

At 4 a.m., Maggie went into the closet where Matthew had left her dominatrix outfit and riding crop. With difficulty, she managed to fasten the black stockings to the attached garters. Her breasts were falling out of the bustier's demi-cups. Holding the riding crop she admired her reflection in the mirror. The only detail left was to secure John to the bed. Fortunately, Matthew had earlier attached the restraints.

At 5 a.m., Maggie retired the crop, un-restrained John, and fell back asleep. Two hours later she woke up, threw on a robe over the outfit she still wore, and found John making coffee.

John said in a chipper tone, "Good Morning. I just cleared my schedule."

"What would you like to do?"

"Go to your gallery, I understand Matthew has one of your paintings there."

Maggie shook her head, "John...you really don't want to see it."

"Let's go back to my place. I want to shower and change clothes. We can get to the gallery when it opens. Now, get some clothes on. Actually, come here first. I want to see what you have on underneath your robe."

John removed her robe and said, "Turn around. Nice. I like what you did with the riding crop handle."

"You were asleep."

He slapped her bare bottom and said, "Now, run along and get dressed before I change my mind and tie you to the bed."

At the gallery, Matthew pulled her aside. "How was last night?"

"Perfect."

As John walked around the gallery, both Maggie and Matthew admired how sexy John looked in his button fly jeans and V-neck cashmere sweater.

Matthew said, "Handsome."

Maggie gave him a stern look. "Stay away from him. This is my second warning."

"Just keep an open mind. We could always share him."

On the back wall hung the fifty-five-inch by eighty-five-inch oil on canvas titled Meliades. Matthew and Maggie watched as John moved towards it.

"Are you nervous, Cinderella? Prince Charming sounds like a nice guy."

"I'm scared the magical spell will go away."

Looking at her painting, she vividly remembered how lustful she felt while being photographed. Sean had posed her leaning against a large, live oak tree. Her head tilted down with her face partially hidden by her waist length auburn hair. Sean intentionally tore open the thin linen cover-up she wore, revealing her pale skin and rosy nipples. Her left hand squeezed her right nipple while her right hand was buried between her legs. He insisted that she masturbate while he took the photos. The lighting was perfect; the afternoon sun focused on her left hand while a soft shadow obscured on her right hand.

Matthew had walked over to John. Maggie moved in closer, eavesdropping on their conversation.

"I want to buy it," John said.

"I'm afraid it's not on the market. It's in my private collection."

"Matthew, everything has a price. I understand the other two paintings each sold for twenty-five thousand dollars. Since this is the last one in the collection, I'll offer you thirty-five thousand dollars."

Maggie walked over as John announced, "Then we have a deal?"

Maggie said, "What did I miss? What deal?"

Matthew replied, "Your friend is a hard negotiator. I'm selling Meliades to him for thirty-five thousand dollars."

Maggie was stunned as she turned to John, "Are you crazy?"

"Not at all; I feel once you reestablish yourself in the art world, the painting will only go up in value."

"You're taking a gamble in that regard," she said.

"I don't gamble; I take calculated risks. It's an investment I feel confident about."

"Glad it's your money and not mine."

"Matthew, can you ship it to my condo in California?"

Matthew replied, "No problem."

John turned back to Maggie and said, "I want you to come visit me in San Francisco and help me decide where to hang it."

Maggie said, "Perhaps over your toilet since you just flushed a lot of money down the drain."

After finishing up at the gallery, they walked a block to one of Maggie's favorite French bistros, Little Prince. Maggie had emptied her glass of Chardonnay and was noticing how John had been silent for a minute while staring at her. As she unconsciously fidgeted with her unruly hair, she smiled and broke the silence.

"What...what are you thinking of right now?"

"Your artistic talent amazes me. You've married Impressionism with eroticism. It reminds me of Auguste Renoir's work."

"I was fortunate to land an art history internship at the Barnes Foundation. They have 181 of Renoir's paintings."

"Artistically, your work is complex and masterfully executed."

"You're too kind, but thank you. As I told you previously, it was an uncensored time in my life."

"What inspired you to paint *The Nymphs* series?"

"It started out being a joke. Sean and I were visiting with my friend, Ron, at his cottage in Magnolia Springs, Alabama. We all had gotten high when Sean suggested that I pose for him as various mythological nymphs. We'd just gotten back from Greece where he had done a story on Greek mythology.

"We learned that nymphs are generally classified into three different types: land, water, and tree. There were several beautiful live oaks on Ron's property, so Sean photographed me first as *Meliades*, the nymph of oak trees. I next posed as *Hesperus*, a land nymph, in the garden where Ron's Satsuma tree was loaded with ripe citrus fruit. I then waded nude in the river and posed as *Naiad*. The sun was starting to set, casting a beautiful reflection in the Magnolia River.

"After we returned to Chicago, Sean went away on a seven-week assignment. Bored, I started looking at the photos he'd taken and painted the series. The last one I painted was the one you bought from Matthew, *Meliades*. An undisclosed art collector bought the other two at my opening exhibit."

"What happened to all the photographs he took of you?"

"When I left him, I took them and the negatives with me. For months, I seethed with anger until finally Matthew visited me and intervened. We built a bonfire on the beach and burned them all. I hoped that would finally end that chapter of my life."

"I know just what Maggie O' needs. How about some shopping therapy to cheer you up? The fantasy role-playing has made me want to go shopping with you."

"That sounds fun. There are two stores that Matthew and I missed yesterday, Agent Provocateur and The Pleasure Chest."

"You took Matthew shopping with you?"

"Yes, he knew where to go."

"Did you let him see you in those provocative outfits?"

Maggie sensed possible jealousy. "It's not like he hasn't seen my body before. Until now he owned a large nude painting of me." She blurted, "As a matter of fact, he picked out the outfits that I wore."

"In that case, I want to take you shopping for all new things. I've no desire to see you in anything Matthew or any other man for that matter picked out for you."

"Even my pearl thong?"

"Just don't wear it around me. Wear it around Matthew."

They first stopped at The Pleasure Chest, a well-known West Village adult store. John said, "Let's see if we can find where the restraints are."

"I already have one."

"Give it to Matthew."

At their next stop, Agent Provocateur, John found Maggie the perfect replacement dress, the *Thora Dress,* inspired by Dior's New Look of the 1940's. Designed to sculpt the curves of the body, it fit Maggie's curves perfectly. While the front suggested a dominant boardroom look, the back laced up like a French corset.

When Maggie modeled it for John, he commented, "You should wear this at the opening of your next art exhibit."

"You're so optimistic."

"Now, I want to pick out some lingerie."

An attractive sales clerk noticed them looking at a bra in the Jena Collection; she asked them, "What size do you need?"

"36C."

"Do you want to try the briefs or the thong?"

John took control over the conversation and responded, "I find these briefs quite sexy because of the hooks and eyes down the front and in the rear."

Maggie saw her input was unimportant as the clerk responded back to John, "I'll bring her the matching suspenders. What color would you like?"

John answered, "Black."

The clerk asked, "Would you like to go for a color in the stockings? I recommend the champagne with red seams."

John agreed, "Yes."

John was already at the register when Maggie finished dressing, walked over to the cashier, and pulled out her Amex card.

The clerk said, "Your friend has already taken care of it."

Agitated, Maggie turned to John, "You shouldn't have."

John replied, "Take it out on me later in bed when you flog me."

The sales clerk smiled.

Maggie asked, "And what's in your shopping bag?"

"A surprise for later."

John put the shopping bags on the floor and pressed Maggie against the elevator wall. As the elevator door closed, his lips stayed pressed against hers, and he hooked two fingers inside her bringing her to climax before the door opened on the thirty-ninth floor.

"Was that so bad?"

"Can we go down to the lobby and try that again?"

"I can tell your fear of heights can be sensually used to my advantage."

As he unlocked his door, he said, "I want to cook tonight."

"You like to cook?"

"I get tired of eating out. There is a neighborhood market I walk to."

"So what's for dinner?"

"I'm thinking seafood, depending on what they have fresh today. Here is something for you."

John handed Maggie an Agent Provocateur box; inside was a black see-thru kimono.

"This will look great over your new lingerie. Why don't you take a bath and put on your new lingerie and robe while I run to the market."

John entered the bathroom holding a glass of wine and wearing a bibbed apron with *Taste My Sausage* boldly imprinted on it.

Maggie laughed. "Where on Earth did you get that apron?"

"It was a housewarming present."

"I would love to taste your sausage. Is that what you've planned for dinner?"

"Save that thought for later. I need to start cooking before I get distracted."

"Wow", John said, "Turn around. You're such a temptress in that outfit."

He had put on some music. Maggie said, "Divinyls, *I Touch Myself*, I love this song. Your taste in music surprises me."

Later that evening, he led her into the bedroom. Removing her kimono, he unhooked the front eyehook freeing her full breasts. He opened the bedside drawer. "Sit at the edge of the bed; I've a surprise for you.

As Maggie unwrapped it, he said, "It's a double cuff to restrain your hands.

53

Maggie read the inscription aloud, "As I am, you were. As I was, you will be." Looking up at John she said, "This relates to a painting, *The Holy Trinity* by Masaccio."

"Hand them to me."

John cuffed her hands behind her back.

John woke her up at seven thirty with a mug of coffee in his hand. "It's time to get up, Maggie O'."

She opened her eyes and smiled at him in his business attire. "You look handsome. Are you meeting a female client today?"

"As a matter of fact I am, a Chief Operating Officer."

"Um hum. She's probably attractive?"

"Perhaps twenty years ago. And what artist are you courting today?"

"I'm meeting Sharon Sullivan at Café Boulud. She came in late last night from California. She's the artist we're having the reception for on Friday."

"I'll be in the living room getting my paperwork organized."

Maggie had borrowed John's flannel robe. He wrapped his arms around her and started kissing her. Barefoot, she had to stand on her tiptoes to reach his lips.

"Here, let me help you." He lifted her to the counter, the perfect level to kiss her. He untied her sash and fondled her breasts. Sliding his right hand inside her, he could tell she was wet with desire.

"I'm sorry I have to leave you like this. Why don't you get Buzz out and let him finish what I started. I'll text you later."

As he walked out the door, Maggie said, "You can be cruel; do you know that?"

CHAPTER SIX

PIZZA NIGHT

Riding in the taxi to Café Boulud, she noticed that John had sent her a text.

"Order the Winter Squash Soup and the Belgian Endive Salad. Water with lemon."

"Thanks for researching the menu for me."

"If these negotiations go well, I can leave here at a reasonable hour. What would you like to do for dinner?"

"I'm craving Sicilian pizza. Could we bend the rules and have one?"

"I'll think about it. Need to refocus on the meeting. Hopefully, I'll see you soon."

Maggie found Sharon waiting for her at the bar. She greeted her petite friend with a tender hug. Sharon handed her a gift bag and said, "Happy Belated Birthday."

Inside the bag, Maggie found a box of note cards. The picture on the card was a painting of Maggie sunning on the beach in Puerto Vallarta. She and Sharon had spent their Christmas holidays there.

"You painted me?"

"Not quite as erotically as you paint yourself. I hope you like it since you're the one who inspired me to live in the moment."

"You've got that wrong; you're a master at living in the moment. By the way, thanks for convincing me to end my sabbatical."

55

"Sounds like my suggestion worked. Fill me in on the details."

After lunch, Maggie went back to John's condo and started responding to the flood of emails in her inbox. She gazed at the Empire State Building lights from the window and looked at the time on her phone. *I can't believe it's five already.* She heard a key opening the door and eagerly waited for John to enter.

He said, "Special delivery."

Recognizing the pizza box, she said, "I love Jiannetto's."

John disappeared into the kitchen. "I'll put the pizza on warm so we can relax for a while. I splurged on this special Chianti. Let me open it so it can breathe, then I want to change."

Maggie stood up and stretched. Dressed in black yoga pants and a tight-fitting white tank top, she said, "I should change too."

"No need to. Just relax and turn on some music."

She found a Jazz channel and waited on the sofa.

John changed into gray sweatpants and a Berkeley t-shirt.

"So you went to Berkeley?"

"I got my undergraduate degree there."

"Have you always lived in California?"

"Actually, I grew up here in New York. After I graduated from Harvard, I practiced law at my dad's West 52nd Street firm for seven years. Let's try the Chianti."

Lifting her up onto the kitchen counter, he pulled off her yoga pants and thong.

"What do you think you're doing?"

He gave her an impish grin. Trying to sound Italian he said, "This Chianti was grown in my family's vineyard in Tuscany. We have this tradition that is done before the wine ages."

"What is it?"

John drizzled Chianti between her legs.

She said, "I can't believe you poured your wine there."

"Now, I must lick it off of you."

After a minute of his licking, Maggie started liking his imaginary game.

"I must tend to your most sacred spot to please the wine goddess."

"You're going to make me ..."

John stopped. "I'm not finished licking all the wine off. I must take care of that before you can come. If you climax then, tannins will be at the perfect level resulting in ripe and rich tasting Chianti."

"And what happens if I can't climax?"

"You will be kicked out of my bed forever."

Fortunately, a climax resulted; the Chianti would be outstanding, her place in his bed saved.

"That's an excellent Chianti don't you think?" he said.

Maggie sat up and replied, "I must say I've never been to a wine tasting like this one."

"Let me pour you some. It's one of the better Chiantis, a 2001 Chianti *Classico Riserva*. Would you like some pizza to go with it?"

"Only if it goes in my mouth."

"It certainly spices things up a bit. Do you have a favorite sexual fantasy?"

"I guess it would be having sex with two men at the same time."

"I have to call my partner in San Francisco to discuss the meeting I had today. I'll probably be busy with work for a half-hour, then I want to take a quick shower. Be waiting for me in the bedroom. Wear the black kimono and have Buzz and friends ready."

Maggie was checking her email when John brought in Chianti filled Riedel tumbler.

"Sorry, the call took longer than I thought it would. Wait a minute; you broke one of my house rules?"

Confused, Maggie replied, "I did? What?"

"Never work in the bedroom. Bedrooms are for two things, sleep and sex. Notice I don't have a TV in here."

"Sorry. I didn't see your rules posted. Besides, I would rather have you in bed with me than this laptop anytime. I will immediately remove it from the bedroom so it won't interfere with the *feng shui* of the room."

"I'm going to *feng shui* you in a minute."

"Sounds kinky."

"Hold that thought. I want to take a quick shower."

After his shower, John returned finding Maggie sound asleep.

.

At midnight Maggie woke up and went into the guest bathroom. Staring into the mirror she thought, *It's for the best that I'm leaving to go home Saturday. I'm starting to like this Stranger.* She put on John's robe and found him watching CNN. The pizza box was on the coffee table.

"Sit down and have some pizza."

She replied, "Thanks. Let me grab some water."

"I take it you don't want any more Chianti?"

She returned with water and sat on the sofa.

John turned off the television. "Tell me about Sharon."

"You will love her. I met her when I took her yoga class at a spa retreat in Napa. When she was only thirty-eight, she was diagnosed with breast cancer and had a double mastectomy. She had just turned forty when we met. While battling her cancer, a friend encouraged her to take an art class. She paints with a whimsical style and always has a pink ribbon incorporated in it. I fell in love with her work. It took me six months to convince her to share her art with others.

"An oncologist from Stanford read an article that I wrote on how art healed Sharon. Last month, he was in town for a meeting and came by to see her work. He was so touched by it that he bought the original sixty pieces she'd painted while she was recovering. He plans on displaying them at his clinic."

"Good for her."

"She recently started another series called, *In the Moment.* We'll also be featuring those twelve new paintings."

"I can't wait to meet her. I'm not sure what time I'll be able to be there."

"I know it will be your last night in New York, and I've monopolized your time all week. Please don't feel pressured to come."

"I want to come. It's our last night together. You look bothered. Are you unhappy about something?"

Maggie turned away and replied, "I'm okay."

John turned her head back towards him and looked her directly in the eye. "Look at me right now."

As she looked back, he said, "Like you, I'm confused and bewildered about what has happened these past five nights. I've no intentions of letting you get on a plane Saturday and then never seeing you again. I'm serious about you coming to San Francisco and helping me decide where to hang your painting. And I will be at your exhibition this summer. Now get ready to pucker up. I want to share this wonderful Chianti with you."

John took a drink of Chianti and kissed her.

Maggie said, "Then I guess we aren't strangers anymore?"

Maggie was busy organizing the last minute details of the night's event. This was the first charity event the gallery had hosted. Invitations for the event were sent to patron art collectors, art dealers, well-known charity benefactors, oncologists, hospital administrators, and hospital board members from around the region. Sharon insisted on donating fifty percent of her exhibit commissions back to the Art Heals Cancer Foundation that she had established for breast cancer victims. In addition, Maggie and Matthew agreed to give fifty percent of the gallery's commissions to Sharon's foundation.

Before the guests arrived, Matthew, Sharon, and Maggie sampled a glass of the pink Prosecco. Sharon wore a flattering Kay Unger hot pink sleeveless jacquard cocktail dress that she and Maggie found at Neiman's. Matthew looked like a model in his prized black Armani suit, which he wore with a pastel pink dress shirt and a burgundy paisley silk bow tie that Maggie had given him for Christmas.

Matthew said, "Maggie, where did you find such a sultry dress?"

"John bought it for me at Agent Provocateur."

Sharon's sixty paintings, each embossed with her signature pink ribbon, were displayed on the expansive wall where Maggie's *Meliades* painting once hung. For maximum exposure, Matthew showcased Sharon's new *In the Moment* series next to the bar.

At Maggie's suggestion, the caterer had used a pink theme for the evening: pink Prosecco, pink cocktails, smoked salmon canapés, boiled shrimp with pink rémoulade sauce, prosciutto and melon, and strawberry fudge truffles. The servers dressed in all black and wore pink carnation boutonnières. A harpist played baroque music.

Maggie worked the crowd with ease, promoting Sharon and the other gallery artists. When John arrived, she was engaged in conversation with an oncologist from Manhattan who was interested in commissioning Sharon to do work for his new office. John immediately zeroed in on the back of her seductive dress, grabbed a glass of Prosecco and continued to watch

Maggie as she worked. He could tell by the man's body language and facial expressions that he was attracted to Maggie; what man wouldn't be? He was becoming too familiar with her, touching her lower back and leaning closely into her. She backed away from him, turned around, and made eye contact with John. She had this guilty grimace on her face, as though she had been caught doing something wrong. He adored how she swayed her hips as she walked towards him.

"Thank you for coming tonight."

"And miss the debut of your new dress."

"I hope you don't mind me wearing it."

"I'm flattered that you chose to wear it tonight. Now introduce me to Sharon."

After John was introduced to Sharon, he asked Maggie, "Is that a painting of you lying on the beach?"

"Sharon and I spent this past New Years in Puerto Vallarta. Excuse me; I need to introduce Sharon to someone. I'll be back in a minute."

After she had introduced Sharon to the doctor from Manhattan, she noticed Matthew talking to John as she walked back.

Matthew said, "The reception is almost over. Why don't you two go ahead and leave. You both have early planes to catch." He turned to John and said, "I'll have both paintings shipped to you by next Thursday."

As Matthew turned to greet a client, Maggie whispered to John, "What other painting did you buy?"

"The painting of you on the beach."

Matthew focused back on Maggie and John.

Maggie said, "Matthew, if you don't mind, I think we will. Let me go tell Sharon goodbye."

When Maggie returned, she saw John and Matthew shaking hands as if they had made a pact. She gave Matthew a hug and said, "Thank you, Matthew. You were such a big help this week."

As John unlocked his condo door, he said, "That dress was designed with your incredible body in mind. Speaking of which, did you have a chance to eat anything tonight other than a canary?"

"What do you mean by a canary?"

"Your expression, when I caught you flirting with that man tonight."

"I wasn't flirting."

"Let's change clothes, and I'll make you an omelet."

"I'm afraid I need some help unlacing the back of my dress."

"I love how your breasts look in this dress and how easily I can pull it down and kiss them."

"Sir, I may pass out if I don't eat something."

"I certainly don't want you to pass out on me tonight. Turn around. How did you get this laced up earlier?"

"Matthew helped me."

She winced when John swatted her on the butt.

"You deserve more than that; now change into your domme outfit."

"I thought you didn't want me to wear anything I bought that day."

"I was acting a little jealous. I had a long talk with Matthew tonight. I know he still loves you, and he would jump your bones in a second, but he wants most of all to see you happy again."

"Matthew is like a brother to me."

"Do you have a habit of sleeping with your brother? There you're unlaced. I suggest you hurry out of here and finish undressing before I pin you to the wall."

"Can I wear my pearl thong?"

He gave her his sexy grin and said, "I almost forgot about that. Yes."

She changed into her black Ophelia bustier and black Brachi thong. Since the bustier had garters, she put her hose back on. She had brought a see-through black shirt that she usually wore with a camisole, then changed her mind; the bustier would look sexier under it. It had tiny buttons all the way down the front and on the cuffs of the sheeves. She left it unbuttoned just below her breasts.

The pearl strands aroused her as she walked into the kitchen. John had changed into his Berkeley T-Shirt and sweat pants. As he chopped spinach and mushrooms for the omelet, Maggie walked up behind him and rubbed her body up against him.

"You better stop that or you'll be eating something other than an omelet."

Maggie said, "Let's have a glass of wine. I believe we still have an open bottle in the refrigerator."

She poured the wine and sat down at the counter.

John said, "I admire what you're doing with Sharon's artwork, giving such a high percentage of your commissions to cancer research."

"That was the easy part; I lost my mother to breast cancer."

"I'm sorry to hear that. You don't talk about your family much."

"My parent's divorced when I was five. I later suspected my dad had an affair, but it was kept such a dark secret, in order not to tarnish our stellar reputation."

"Do you take after your mother?"

"I wish. She had that Liz Taylor look about her with her mesmerizing sapphire eyes and jet-black hair. She was petite with a voluptuous body that attracted the attention of every man. I took after my dad's Irish heritage, with his light auburn hair and slight freckles."

"Did you have a close relationship with your mother?"

"Never. She had a thing for younger men. For several summers, she invited one of her boyfriends to stay at our beach cottage. He was closer to my age than hers."

"Is your dad still alive?"

"He lives in Santa Fe with his third wife. They have a seven-year-old son."

"Do you have any other brothers or sisters?"

"No."

"You mentioned your grandparents left you a trust."

"They died in a hit and run automobile accident leaving their entire estate, including their beach cottage, in an irrevocable trust benefiting me. I was their only grandchild. My mother was resentful."

"Why was that?"

"They left a note explaining that they disapproved of her lifestyle and they wanted to protect me. They appointed an attorney to manage my trust. I suspect my mother carried on an affair with him. She used the excuse that she had to meet with him every week about my trust fund. He was by her bedside when she died."

"I don't mean to change the subject, but Matthew told me my paintings will be shipped to me by Thursday. What's your schedule the next few weeks?"

"This coming week, I've an appointment in Birmingham on Tuesday. The following week, on Wednesday, Sharon and I are going to Dr. Robert's clinic in Stanford to hang the paintings. He has a reception planned the following Friday night to unveil Sharon's work."

"I'll be out of town Tuesday as well. How about I fly you in on Friday, and you plan on staying until after Sharon's show?"

"That's over a weeks stay."

"Why don't you do some marketing while you're in San Francisco?"

"It's interesting that you say that; Matthew and I've talked about opening another gallery on the West Coast."

"So you can do your due diligence while you stay with me."

"I don't want to impose on you again. I'll get a hotel room this time."

"When does having wild and crazy sex impose on someone?"

She smiled at him and said, "You know what I mean."

"Let's eat so you can impose on me tonight."

The omelet hit the spot. John insisted on cleaning the dishes. Maggie hopped back on the cold granite counter and asked, "What kind of ritual have you planned for tonight?"

"None; just a simple *us* night--no props and no toys."

"Then why did you want me to wear this outfit?"

"Because you look so hot in it. I'm dying to take it off of you."

John walked over to Maggie and said, "First I want to practice kissing some more. I think I'm close to getting the technique down."

He kissed the back of her neck and then her forehead, eyes, and cheeks. He instinctively knew how to stimulate her passion, slowly and delicately.

He said, "It's time to go to the bedroom, so I can continue kissing all of you."

They each helped the other undress. Maggie was left wearing only her black Bracli pearl thong.

When they had sexual intercourse, Maggie enjoyed John's seemingly alternate personality. His wild animal lust satisfied her masochist need for pleasure and pain, and then afterwards how quickly he reverted back to his tender gentle self.

John rolled over sideways on the bed with his head propped up. "Come lie next to me."

Maggie cuddled up next to him.

John nibbled on her ear and kissed the back of her neck. "I enjoyed how you seduced me with your tongue at Hotel Elysée."

"Why do you excite me so much?"

"Because you've worn an emotional chastity belt far too long; fortunately I found the key."

His words penetrated her innermost fears, peeling away the scar tissue that had imprisoned a part of her. She felt like Inanna, the Sumerian goddess of sexual love, fertility, and warfare who descended into the underworld where her clothing and jewelry were taken from her, thus stripping her of her power. This stranger had rescued her from the underworld and brought her back to reality.

John asked, "What are you thinking?"

"Your comment about an emotional chastity belt hit home for some reason."

"Look, we have been so fortunate to have such incredible sex during this week, but we skipped getting to know each other emotionally. Since we're no longer sexual strangers, we need to start focusing on learning about our more fragile sides."

"I can't imagine you having a fragile side."

"You're wrong. While I usually dress in full armor, I'm still vulnerable; it's like what happened in the Atlanta Airport. This hot redheaded Southern chick sat across from me. I couldn't concentrate on anything else. Fortunately, Mother Nature became our matchmaker, and our flight was cancelled."

.

CHAPTER SEVEN

BITTERSWEET HOME ALABAMA

To Maggie, her flight back home felt like an eternity. She pulled out the lavender scented letter and admired how Chris had used a fountain pen to write it meticulously.

My Dearest Mermaid,

Hope you had a Happy Birthday. I can hardly believe you're thirty-two. Where did the years go? I've followed your success as an artist and am so proud of your accomplishments.

Not a day passes that I don't think about you. How wrong it was for me to have kissed your nymph-like breasts that day. Something about you tempted me, perhaps the purity of your innocence, such a contrast to the vixen ways of your mother.

There is so much I need to explain to you; please find it in your heart to contact me.

I'll always love you,

Chris

A hornet's nest stirred inside her; this couldn't be about the summers they spent together. Not knowing how to deal with it, she had tried to bury this early chapter of her life. She whispered to herself, "Damn it, Chris. Why now?"

Maggie was only thirteen when she met Christopher, her mother's latest twenty-three year old lover. An associate professor at Emory University in Atlanta, Chris was an aspiring author. To young Maggie, he was prince-like with his flax blond hair, ocean blue eyes, and irresistible smile. Originally from Cairns, Australia, his accent sounded exotic and mysterious to the young Alabama teenager who had never traveled abroad. He was a good sport and would play along with her, pretending to be Prince Eric as she assumed the role of Ariel in *The Little Mermaid*. Chris would hold her snug against him as they jumped over the waves together. She felt secure and protected as she clung to his muscular chest; her arms wrapped around his neck and her long legs locked around his waist. One afternoon, as they looked for shells in the water, Maggie was stung high on her inner thigh by a jellyfish. Her hero, Chris, carefully removed the venom sacs with a credit card and washed the area with salt water, followed by a tender kiss on the sting. A warmness stirred in her loin—a stirring she had only experienced alone at night when she slipped her hands beneath the sheets.

As she landed at Pensacola Airport, she was melancholy instead of relieved to be back home. She told herself to snap out of it. Feeling suffocated, she cracked her window as she drove to her West Beach cottage. *It's so nice to breathe the salt air once again.*

Pouring herself a glass of wine, she sat on the screened porch gazing at the Gulf of Mexico. It was five o'clock and also high tide. The pumpkin colored sun was setting in the West, such a beautiful contrast to the teal water and white powder sand. The pounding waves pushed the salt water near the protective dunes that were built after Hurricane Ivan.

After a second glass of wine, she still could not stop thinking about this stranger whom she had allowed into her life; and now on top of that, the note she had received from Chris. Her cell phone pinged.

"I left my heart in New York."

She chuckled to herself thinking what a dry sense of humor John had, and immediately texted back.

"I don't think the lyrics work."

After they had finished texting, she had a severe case of the sexual blues. She gathered her courage to begin reading Chris's new novel. She was relieved when she found it next to the bronze mermaid statue that Chris had once given her for her fifteenth birthday. A sculptor friend of Chris's modeled the mermaid after Maggie.

Written like a fairy tale, it was a coming-of-age story, loosely based on her relationship with Chris. She immersed herself, wondering how he would end the story. She wished his *happily ever after* version had been the truth.

Around 2 a.m., Maggie finished the book. Sleepless, she recalled her summers spending time at the beach with Chris. She and Chris would swim in the mid-afternoon to cool off from the heat. Chris loved the water as much as Maggie. Her mother, Wanda, never joined them; she couldn't stand to get sand on her pedicured toes.

Towards the end of the summer of 1998, fifteen year-old Maggie was diving off Chris's shoulders when her bikini top came untied and washed away in the water. Embarrassed, she didn't know what to do. They were alone; Wanda and Bessie, the housekeeper, were not at the house. Chris carried sobbing Maggie to the shore and wrapped her in a beach towel.

"You have nothing to be embarrassed about; you're beautiful." Chris then eased the towel down and started kissing her awakened nipples.

She had never been kissed on the lips before and certainly not on her breasts. She squirmed beneath his touch, finding his leg and drawing it up between her own, she writhed and ground against him. She didn't want to stop. They swore to each other it would be their little secret.

The next morning, Chris surprised Wanda when he left two weeks early to go back to Atlanta. Saddened, Maggie knew why he had left.

Like both her grandmother and her mother, Maggie spent her high school years at Baylor School, a prominent private boarding school located in Chattanooga, Tennessee. The summer after her sophomore year, Maggie had turned sixteen and grown two inches taller. Her once lanky body was developing into her mother's hourglass shape. She was gravely disappointed to find out that Chris would not be staying with them that summer. He was teaching a summer abroad program in England. With no chance of seeing Chris, Maggie stayed at school during that summer.

It was Monday afternoon and Maggie sat outside on the porch drinking sweet ice tea and watching the waves break. John was on his way home when he called her.

He asked her, "So how was your day?"

"Almost caught up. I'm leaving early tomorrow for Clanton, Alabama. I've a lunch appointment and then I'm heading to Tuscaloosa for a business dinner with a former art professor. He often refers his students to our gallery."

"Have you ever slept with this professor?"

"Why would you even ask such a question?"

"To see how you react."

Maggie arrived at the Main Street Café in Clanton, one of her favorite spots to indulge in Southern country cooking. She was happy to see fried chicken on the daily menu along with her favorite side dishes, creamed potatoes, green beans, and cornbread. John would not approve of her menu choices. For dessert they featured bread pudding; she would go back on a diet tomorrow.

Frank Jones was a soft-spoken, fifty-five-year-old welder who, unfortunately, lost his Birmingham job due to corporate cutbacks. Never married, he moved back to his parent's Chilton County peach farm. In an empty barn, he started making sculptures out of various unused farm implements he found. His girlfriend suggested he sell his work at the various arts and crafts fairs. In October 2013, Maggie met them at the Gulf Shores Shrimp Festival and was impressed with his work. She had been trying to convince him to let her represent him ever since.

"Frank, we're still interested in representing you."

"Miss O'Reilly, I need money. I've applied for every welding job I can find around here. Fortunately, I'm able to live and work on my parents' farm."

"Please call me, Maggie, and say yes this time. I've connections that could get you some large corporate commissions. Art from salvage materials is really in demand. We have another artist moving on to a larger gallery in February; we'll have ample room for several of your sculptures."

"Thank you, Miss O'Reilly, I mean, Miss Maggie, for believing in me. I won't turn you down this time."

After the lunch appointment, Maggie headed to Tuscaloosa. As she pulled into Ron's driveway she pondered, *why do I feel guilty, like a naughty girl?*

Ron greeted her at the door with a way too familiar kiss. Maggie pulled away.

Ron said, "I guess that means you're still not up for a reunion."

"You never stop trying."

"I'm hoping you will change your mind one day. Please come in. It's too early for wine; would you like a cup of ginseng tea?"

"That sounds wonderful. It's quite chilly today."

"You know where the guest room is, if you want to unpack while I make the tea."

Walking to the guest room, she noticed he still had that painting of her at the end of the hall. Ron had painted it right before he took Maggie's virginity. She changed into her yoga pants and a red, V-neck, fleece pullover.

Still remarkably handsome, Ron had recently turned fifty-four. Maggie always remembered his birthday, the twentieth of November, the same day as her grandmother, Mona's birthday. His once coal dark hair had turned an attractive salt and pepper shade. He still wore it back in his signature ponytail. His close-cropped beard and his eyebrows were still dark which framed his lapis blue eyes.

Maggie returned to the living area. "Where do you hide that painting of me when I'm not visiting you?"

"I've never taken it off the wall. It's the best painting I've ever done."

"I can't believe I agreed to model nude for your art classes that year."

"I wish you would let me paint you again. Which gives me an idea for an interesting painting, me painting you as you paint in the nude."

"Professor West, only you would come up with that idea."

"I must say you have a glow about you, that special look of a woman who's being properly shagged."

"I didn't realize you have this ESP gift."

"So you do have someone in your life again. I'm jealous. You know I always enjoyed our time together."

"I also enjoyed our short time together. Admit it; you're so fortunate in your position that you continue to get new interns every year. That must keep your sex life from getting boring."

"Maybe I'm getting too old, but I would rather be in a monogamous relationship, someone who will not leave me as I get harder to live with. You still don't realize how much you meant to me and how difficult it was to let you go."

"You're lying. And besides, it was time for me to go."

"Just remember, there will never be a replacement for you. I understood the best thing was to let you go. Now let's move on before I lose my willpower and try once more to seduce you. So for your benefit, I'll change the subject. Have you started painting again?"

Maggie hesitated before she responded, "Matthew wants me to do another exhibit."

"Your *Nymphs* series was incredible. I remember the weekend you were at my cottage, and you posed for Sean. How you captured his photos of you on canvas was brilliant."

"I was motivated back then."

"I know what motivates you; you're always welcome to stay here."

"You taught me how interconnected sex and painting are."

"Before you learned that, you were just an above average art major. You're the type of artist who must experience passion in your life to express it in your paintings."

"The idea of you painting me as I'm painting in the nude intrigues me. If I do an exhibit, would you consider doing such a painting?"

"I would be delighted. I also expect an invitation to your opening exhibit."

"You will be on my 'A' list."

"Tell me about this new person in your life."

"I met him at the Atlanta airport. Our flight to New York was cancelled."

"It's time to open a bottle of wine. I'll be back in a minute."

Maggie's cell phone vibrated. John had sent a message.

"I suppose you're meeting with Professor Ronald West now."

"Why do you think this?"

73

"I found a nude painting on his website, titled The Virgin. I must say, he captured you well. He also posted a picture he painted of his dock on the Magnolia River, the same location where Sean took those photos of you."

"You're in the wrong profession. You should be a P.I."

"Actually these skills are highly effective in the venture capital industry. We'll discuss how you lost your virginity later."

"That's certainly none of your business."

"Where are you staying tonight?"

"You figure it out."

Ron handed Maggie a glass of wine. "So tell me more; you met him at the Atlanta Airport?"

"I spent the night with him in Atlanta and the rest of the week with him in New York."

"Is this your Reader's Digest Condensed version?"

"All you need to know."

"Is he married?"

"Unless he lied to me, no."

"Are you going to see him again?"

"I fly out to San Francisco on Friday."

Ron smiled at Maggie and said, "I'm happy you've found someone to bring passion back into your life."

"Thank you. That means a lot, especially coming from you. Are you seeing anyone special?"

"A new professor in our department. She's near my age, fifty. Divorced with grown kids, a lot of fun out of bed. Unfortunately, her bedroom skills are lacking, but we're working on it."

"You're a wonderful teacher. I'm sure you'll remedy that."

Maggie woke up hung-over. She rolled over to make sure she was alone in bed. She and Ron consumed three bottles of wine the night before with the Greek-style lamb chop dinner he had prepared. In his inebriated state, he had persisted in wanting to sleep with her. For the first time, she stood her ground with him. She looked at her phone; John had texted several times during the night. *Oh, shit. He's probably mad that I didn't respond. I need to get back to the beach so I can pack for my trip, if I'm still welcome.*

Maggie kissed Ron goodbye at seven and was two hours into her drive when her cell phone rang. She hesitated before answering. Trying to sound chipper she said, "Good Morning."

"Good Morning. How was your evening?"

"Totally platonic, if that's what you want to know."

"Unfortunately, I have to send a limo to pick you up at the airport. I'll be in a meeting Friday afternoon. I hope to be home around six. Make yourself at home when you get there."

Maggie's friend, Mary, had offered to drive Maggie to the Pensacola Airport. In the hour drive, Maggie told Mary the details of the last two weeks.

Mary said, "It's about time. I'm happy you have finally found someone to be romantically involved with."

"Did I say romantically involved? I don't think he's the type that wants a romantic relationship; he's paying alimony to three ex-wives. Believe me, I know I'm going to get burned again, but he is so damn good in bed."

"My Phi Pi little sister, Carla, is finally getting married, and Susie just had a baby girl."

"So how many babies does this make for our sorority now?"

"I think this makes number fourteen; I'll have to check my computer spreadsheet."

"We're so fortunate to have you as our chapter historian, tallying our weddings, divorces, and children. I'm surprised you don't track our orgasms."

The limo driver brought Maggie to John's Vallejo Street condo located in the Pacific Heights district. The contemporary decorated condo was stunning with its striking wide-planked ebony hardwood floors. The spacious raised living room and dining room area had a gas log fireplace and floor to ceiling sliding doors that opened to a large private deck. Because the condo was located on the third floor, it had an unobstructed view of the Golden Gate Bridge and the Bay.

Maggie was drawn to John's black and white photography collection. She tried to see who the artist was but couldn't find a signature. They looked like the famous photographer, Ansel Adams' work.

The kitchen was sleek with white cabinets, stainless steel appliances, and black granite counter tops. Two leather and chrome bar stools were pulled up to the counter. Everything was immaculate, no clutter, in contrast to the shabby chic coastal style that Maggie was accustomed to.

Peeking inside the refrigerator, she found it stocked with fruit, vegetables, and other healthy things. There wasn't a mayonnaise jar to be found. Thirsty, she grabbed a mineral water bottle.

There were two bedrooms; the largest one had a private bath with an oversized walk-in shower. The smaller bedroom had a more modest private bathroom.

Her cell phone was ringing in the kitchen; she hurried to answer it.

"So you're at the condo?"

"I love your place. Where would you like me to put my things?"

"Use the guest room closet and bath."

John arrived earlier than she expected. She was in the shower, listening to Adele singing *Set Fire to the Rain* on her phone and had left open the bathroom door. John was amused by her private performance as he listened to Maggie sing along as she shaved her legs. He stripped naked and opened the glass door startling her.

As she started to scream, he silenced her with a welcoming kiss.

"You startled me. You weren't supposed to be here until later."

"I shortened the meeting so I could be with you."

Maggie firmly grasped his cock and said, "I'm glad you did. I missed this."

"Be patient. Turn around. Let me wash your back for you. Then we'll go in the bedroom. I want you to get familiar with the setting before we decide where your paintings need to be hung."

"Where are the paintings?"

"They're in my storage room. Every time I looked at them, I wanted you."

CHAPTER EIGHT

PICTURE HANGING

John pushed Maggie down on the bed. Normally, she would be more patient and relish the pleasure of foreplay, but as she clawed at his back, she begged him, "I want you so."

"Get on your hands and knees at the edge of the bed."

After several intense minutes, John withdrew his fully erect cock. She collapsed backwards on the bed. As she anticipated the second erotic act, she delighted in how sex with John was like an orchestrated symphony. The first movement is brisk and lively; the second movement is slower and more lyrical; the third movement is an energetic minuet; and the fourth is a rollicking finale.

Feeling alive and awakened again, Maggie sat down at the counter bar in front of a glass of Chardonnay, watching John cutting up fruit and cheese. "I like your condo. It's so clean and uncluttered. I'm especially intrigued by your collection of photos. They remind me of Ansel Adams. I checked to make sure you didn't have some of his work."

"I wish I did; these photos were taken by an amateur."

"I would love to discover this amateur and help launch their career."

"He has other interests right now."

"That's a pity. Such talent wasted. Will you not at least give me a chance at trying to make him consider his options with The Launch?"

"I don't think so."

Surprised by his response Maggie retorted, "Why not? Oh…I get it…you're the photographer. Did you study photography?"

"Just one class in college."

"Did you ever consider photography as a career?"

"My father wanted me to be a lawyer, follow his path."

"How did you end up here?"

"Practicing law never did appeal to me. One of our venture capital clients asked me to join the firm and start a West Coast office."

"Do you still do photography as a hobby?"

"I haven't done anything serious in several years."

Maggie picked up a large framed photograph of two children playing on the beach. "Is this of Jack and Annie?"

"Yes. I took that this Christmas, when we were in Maui."

"They both look just like you."

Maggie's internal clock was still set on central time. At 6 a.m., she was still in bed, but wide-awake thinking where to display Meliades. Although it flattered her to think John wanted it in his bedroom, she wondered how another woman or his children would feel about a portrait of a naked woman intimately touching herself being on display. The perfect solution came to her. There were bookcases on each side of the queen-size bed. If they moved the bed to the opposite wall, then the painting could be hung between the bookcases. A remote controlled decorative screen could be installed to hide it from view when appropriate.

John rolled over and guided her hand to his erect cock. Picture hanging was not important now.

While they ate breakfast, Maggie discussed her idea for rearranging the bedroom. John said, "I like your idea. I could have a king-size bed on the other wall. I hate sleeping in a queen-size bed. I know just the type of bed I want. Let's go shopping today for it."

"Where do you want to go?"

"I'm not sure; I had an interior designer get the furniture I have now."

"Do you have a Room & Board store?"

"In SoMa."

"The painting Sharon did of me on the beach, have you decided where you might want it hung?"

"Most definitely in the foyer, the first thing you see when you enter."

As he drove to the store, John said, "I remember when this store opened. I researched the company and admired their business model. They handcraft their furniture in America. They're green-oriented, using solar energy at their SoMa store."

They parked in front of a large three-story building. Maggie said, "What an unusual building."

"They restored a Chinese import warehouse. Andrea Cochran designed the landscape."

It took no time for John to find the bed he wanted, the Architecture Bed. He admired how it was made of natural steel bars. A female salesperson came over to assist them. She asked him, "What size do you need?"

"A king."

She added, "It also comes in a California King which is four inches longer than the regular king and four inches smaller width wise."

John said, "That's perfect."

"You have one other option. You don't need to use a box spring with this bed, so we offer two different under bed clearances, either eleven and one-half inches or fifteen and one-half inches from the ground. The one you are looking at here is eleven and one-half inches."

John had Maggie sit on the side of the bed and then he kneeled next to her to see where he would hit her sweet spot. He replied, "This will do."

The clerk asked, "So, you want this type of mattress?"

John said, "Yes. Can you deliver today?"

"I'll check."

Maggie said, "I suggest that you consider some nightstands and lamps since you don't have any in the room."

John replied, "Would you pick them out?"

Maggie walked around looking at the various styles of bedside tables. She brought John over to see one she liked and said, "I like the Linear Nightstand. It has a drawer and two shelves. The walnut finish with the natural steel knobs would look great with the bed you picked out. I would rather find some unique lamps for the tables, maybe from the Art Deco period."

In less than an hour, they had finished furniture shopping. Maggie said, "You amaze me. How quickly and efficiently you did that. However, we forgot to shop for bed linens."

"I've a particular place I want to go to; it's near my office."

Samuel Schouor was in the heart of Union Square district on Sutter Street. They both admired the *Biagio* ensemble with its rich metallic tones in gold, pewter and pearl. John requested the entire ensemble to fit the new California King.

They made it back to the condo at two-thirty and waited for the delivery of the bedroom furniture. They had stopped at Boudin Sourdough Bakery & Café to get sandwiches to take back to the condo.

81

Maggie said, "I'm surprised you stopped at a deli today with your restricted diet."

"You have made me bend the rules twice now, first pizza and now sandwiches."

"Isn't it nice to live dangerously for a change?"

"I've been thinking about something totally crazy but at the same time logical."

"What?"

"You and I were only strangers less than two weeks ago. You've stopped painting, and I've stopped photography. I think our paths were meant to cross in other ways than just sharing a bed together. Would you consider letting me photograph you?"

"Why would you want to do that?"

"I think you are incredibly photogenic, and hopefully you might consider using my photos to paint again."

"Understand, I did that before; I was terribly hurt in the end."

"I'm not your *Chicago* con man. Nor am I currently married. I've already revealed my marital history, including children. I want to help you get out of this cold spell you've been in."

"Maybe this would work."

"Even if it doesn't work, we can enjoy ourselves as we try."

The delivery service assembled the bedroom furniture and removed the queen bed. John helped Maggie hang the *Meliades* nymph painting; it fit perfectly between the bookcases.

John said, "Wow, Maggie O', I love it there. It makes an erotic statement."

"I like it too. I think you need something under it to anchor it."

"How about a spanking bench?"

She shook her head in disbelief.

"Don't give me that innocent act. You know you like it when I play a little rough with you. Now, let's get the bed made and try it out."

Maggie threw a new pillow at him. "Any excuse to have sex."

John threw it back to her, "I never need an excuse to have sex and don't you forget it."

"Yes, sir, but let's finish up here first."

As they made the bed, Maggie commented, "The steel lines form a cage-like atmosphere around the bed."

"That's why I like it, perfect for bondage. The height will be great for certain positions I have in mind."

"Stop it. You're making me horny. A stiff breeze makes you horny. Come here. Let's test my theory that the height is right."

John started undressing her. He tossed her jeans, shirt, and thong to the floor. Maggie reciprocated, tossing his jeans and shirt next to her pile. With their armor off, they reverted to their most primal instincts.

John stood at the side of the bed. "Sit on the edge of the bed and spread your legs around me; yes, this could be the perfect height."

He cupped his hands under her buttocks, lifted her up while thrusting inside her. His mouth found her right nipple and sucked and pulled at it, driving her crazy.

She arched her back as John swayed his hips and varied his strokes between long and short. She begged him, "Harder."

After they both had climaxed, Maggie said, "Is the bed height okay?"

John kissed her neck. "I had to think seriously about the height options. I could see advantages for each height. I'm considering putting a higher bed in the guest room."

"You know what, Mr. Kramer, you're part of a unique breed. You are so analytical, yet so sensual, traits that are rare to find in the same person."

"Kind of like you, wouldn't you say?"

"I've been accused of having multiple personalities."

"Would you mind if I get my camera out; you have such a sensual glow right now? Did you bring the black see-thru kimono I bought you?"

"Yes."

"Just wear it and your black stilettos."

The San Francisco Bay had a butterscotch cast to it as the sun was starting to set. John walked outside with his Nikon on the private balcony. The Golden Gate Bridge and the Palace of Fine Arts could be seen in the distance. Maggie stood frozen inside the doorway.

"John said, "I want to take the pictures on the deck.""

"No. I'm scared to go out on your deck."

"You've got to be kidding me. It's just three stories up."

John walked over to Maggie and grabbed her hand. "I'll be right here with you. There's nothing to be frightened of. The deck is completely fenced."

Slowly, they walked over to the limestone block fence. I want you to stand here next to the rail. Turn towards me more and pinch your nipples until they're aroused."

"Hurry, John, I'm starting to hyperventilate."

"You know how I distract you on the elevator; I have an idea. Take off your robe and brace yourself against the rail."

The sun had set, and John removed his sweatpants. He walked over to her and checked to see if she was ready for him.

"Slow down your breathing. This should get your mind off your fear."

Maggie squeezed the rail as he entered her from behind. She couldn't control her breathing.

John was holding her by the hips. As he thrust inside her, he said, "Now let go of the rail."

84

"I can't. I'm afraid."

"That was not a question, that was a command. Let go. I've got you."

When Maggie released her grip, she became lightheaded, as though she were about to faint. It reminded her of when she had experimented with erotic asphyxiation with Sean. Her fear increased when John pulled away from her and immediately she climaxed.

"You can grab the rail now. I want to take some pictures of you from this angle."

Maggie made a spinach, mushroom, and black olive frittata while John worked on the computer editing the photos.

At dinner he said, "I enjoyed that. You're a good cook."

"I have limited cooking skills."

"Let's take our wine over to the sofa and look at the pictures."

Maggie looked at the images on John's laptop. "I love them. They are quite edgy."

"You looked hot. I've never taken a picture with a hard-on. You can tell you're frightened."

"I was petrified. I can't believe you made me do that."

"You enjoyed how it ended."

"It was almost like an erotic asphyxiation."

"You had 'la petite mort' caused by you hyperventilating. You're carbon dioxide levels in the blood fell. Have you done erotic asphyxiation before?"

"Sean liked doing it to himself. On one occasion, I let him do it to me. How about you?"

"It's not my thing. I had a buddy in law school who died that way. Is there a picture you would be willing to paint?"

"The lighting, while too strong for my painting style, works for your photographs."

85

"Softer lighting? I can go back on the computer and make adjustments."

Maggie stood in front of the mirror, combing her freshly washed hair when John knocked on the door.

She opened the door slightly and said, "Yes?"

"Can I take a picture of you now?"

"I'm not presentable; my hair is wet."

"I want to try something different with my camera."

She opened the door wearing a towel wrapped around her body.

"What do you mean you aren't presentable? Even in a white towel you look sexy. Put your leg on the bench and rub it with some lotion."

As she posed, the towel parted at the bottom, exposing her. She tried to close the gap when John stopped her. He slid his index and middle fingers inside her and used his thumb to brush her clit. Maggie's breathing quickened. Removing his fingers, he said, "Now make yourself climax."

Looking through his Nikon lens he captured the whole orgasmic ritual.

"Maggie, check this out. Sit at my desk and look at these. I'll get us some wine."

Maggie walked back in wearing her red cashmere robe. There was a slight chill in the air, and she was glad she had packed it. His new photographs amazed her; it was as though his camera had seduced her.

"What do you think?"

"I'm blown away by how you have captured my emotions in these photos. Maybe it's because I'm the subject. We need an unbiased opinion. What about sending them to Matthew? He'll be totally honest."

"Send them. But don't disclose who took the photos."

An hour later, Matthew sent Maggie a text message.
"Don't tell me you have reunited with Sean again? I thought you were in San Francisco? These photos blew me away."
Maggie winked at John as she texted Matthew back, *"They were taken by a new amateur photographer I've discovered."*
"Doll, do you think he would allow you to use these photos to paint from?"
"I can always ask him."
"How about a double exhibit of his photographs and your paintings?"
"I'll let you know. Goodnight."
"Matthew was impressed by the pictures." There was no reason to tell John yet about Matthew's idea of a double exhibit.

The next morning, she put on her warm red robe and found John at his desk, working on his computer. "You're sure out of bed early this morning."
"I had a project I wanted to finish. Get some coffee. I made a slide show from the photos I took of you last night. Come look at them."
She was caught off-guard as she viewed his erotic photos. "You did this without my permission?"
"I wanted to capture you in this vulnerable natural situation, not something staged."
She was shocked looking at his intimate bondage shots, artistically intrigued by the raw emotions he'd captured in her. She had been blindfolded and did not know he had been taking them.
"I assumed it would be alright with you. You're welcome to delete them."

He tried to reinforce his statement with a sensual kiss and embrace, but Maggie pulled away.

"I've a lot to think about. Perhaps me coming here was not a good idea."

John would not give up as he pulled her back in and forced his kiss upon her. She couldn't resist him, as she wondered what was happening to her--fate or another fatal attraction?

CHAPTER NINE

METAMORPHOSIS

All morning, John walked on eggshells. *Kramer you idiot, why did you do such a crazy thing; she came so close to leaving you.*

He knocked on the bathroom door, and she opened it wearing a towel wrapped around her. He smelled her lavender scented lotion and wanted to pick her up, throw her on the bed, and make passionate love to her. Not sex but make love, a feeling he'd tried to avoid since his nasty last divorce.

"Maggie, I've an idea. It's a beautiful Sunday; let's go for a drive up the coast and have brunch. Pack an overnight bag in case we decide to spend the night somewhere. Also, pack Buzz, the riding crop, and that sexy outfit you wore at Hotel Elysée."

Impossible for her to stay mad at him, she sensed how sorry he was as she seductively walked towards him and placed her hands around his neck. "Are you hinting for me to fulfill your secret fantasy again?"

He reached under her towel and squeezed her buttocks tightly, "What a great idea, but I was thinking of something else I want to use it for." He whacked her bottom and said, "Now get dressed and packed so we can leave soon."

They headed north on US 101 turning onto California State Highway 1, a narrow two-lane roadway that winds between rugged cliffs and the Pacific Ocean. After passing Stinson Beach and Bolinas Lagoon, the road avoided the immediate coastline of Point Reyes National Seashore and headed towards Tomales Bay.

John said, "That's Tomales Bay, an inlet of the Pacific Ocean. They do a lot of oyster farming here. Across the bay, you can see Point Reyes National Seashore."

John surprised Maggie when he pulled up in front of Nick's Cove, a roadside restaurant overlooking the bay. "This place has a fascinating history. A well-known San Francisco restaurateur, Pat Kuleto, purchased it and closed it down for ten years while he restored the cottages and restaurant. He sunk roughly eight million dollars in it. Unfortunately, it was a financial disaster for him. He recently sold it to a group of silent investors.

"Over there are five waterfront cottages that they rent out. They have other cottages as well."

"They look like they belong in the 1930's. Have you ever stayed here before?"

"Several times."

"I doubt you've stayed here alone."

"You're being presumptuous."

"You've made it your business to find out about my past love life. I hardly know much about yours."

"There isn't that much to know. I'll check if they have a cottage available that they can show us."

Maggie realized how he always changed the subject when she questioned him personally.

When he came back, he said, "They have my favorite cottage available, Bandit's Bungalow. We can stay here tonight, if you like? Let's check it out."

"Just a coincidence that they have your favorite cottage available tonight?"

"Isn't it amazing how things can just fall in place?"

"Yeah, right."

The bungalow was charming with light painted paneling, lots of windows that showcased a majestic view of the bay, and a corner wood-burning fireplace. Someone knocked at the door. John opened it and found a perky young woman holding a tray. "Welcome to Nick's. These are our complimentary barbecued oysters and the Roederer Estate, *L'Ermitage* Brut sparkling wine you ordered. Mr. Kramer, would you like me to open it for you now?"

"Just leave it in the bucket."

"Is there anything else I can do for you?"

As he signed the room service receipt, he said, "We're fine. Thank you."

As soon as she left, Maggie said, "This morning you surprised me with those photos you took and now this surprise. I've a good mind to get my riding crop out and try it out on you."

"Promise? How can you still look so beautiful when you're angry? I know just what you need to calm down."

John picked her up and carried her over his shoulder. As he pinned her down on the bed, she tried to resist. *Why do I need him to control me like this?*

After John kissed her, he asked, "Are you calmed down now?"

"As far as my anger goes."

"Since it's pleasant outside, let's sit on the deck and enjoy the oysters and wine. Unless you're afraid of going out on the deck?"

"I don't mind decks over water."

Maggie felt a slight buzz from the wine. Being upset earlier, she had skipped eating breakfast.

"I like the oysters. They are smaller and sweeter than the ones we get on the Gulf Coast."

91

"The water in the Gulf of Mexico is warmer and has more salinity, causing the oysters to mature faster. Why don't we get some brunch so we can go exploring afterward?"

Once they were seated, John said, "I like how the menu features local, seasonal ingredients; do you know what you want to order?"

"Do I get a choice?"

"Still mad at me? I hoped this surprise might make up for the other surprise."

"Kind of like make-up sex?"

Maggie indulged on the Dungeness Crab Benedict and John on his favorite dish, Nick's Cove Paella.

Maggie said, "I can't believe it's already after two."

"Let's take a drive up the coast and find a secluded beach. We can pack a picnic and watch the sunset. We'll stop at the Bodega Country Store on the way."

"Isn't Bodega where they filmed *The Birds*?"

"I'll drive you by the schoolhouse they used in the movie."

At the Bodega Country Store, Maggie looked at all the Alfred Hitchcock memorabilia while John shopped for their picnic. They got back on the Pacific Coast Highway driving north. The road curved quite a bit and Maggie remarked, "I've never been to this part of California. I like how the topography is so unspoiled."

"I love to come up this way; it's such a pleasant change from the city. While it's mostly known for its wonderful wineries, it's a diverse agriculture area with many dairy farms."

He continued, "We're stopping at the head of Bodega Bay. Up on this cliff and during this time of the year, we should see gray whales migrating south for the calving season. I think I see some now. Let me get the binoculars out."

John adjusted the binoculars and handed them to her.

"I see them. Wonder how far they migrate?"

"Round-trip, twelve thousand miles, the longest migration of any mammal on earth, from the Bering Sea to Baja California."

"You're also the migrating type in your business."

"I surpass even the gray whale in the number of miles I travel each year. Let's find a secluded beach."

After several breathtaking highway pull-offs, they came to a pathway where they could walk down to the beach.

John said, "We appear to be alone. During the warmer months, this parking area is packed. When I usually come here, I prefer to spend Sunday night and go back on Monday morning when the traffic dies down."

As they got out of the car, Maggie noticed that John had left his camera on the back seat.

"Don't you want to bring your camera?"

"I don't want to upset you again."

"I've gotten over it. Bring it. You never know, I may want to dance nude on the beach."

"That would be a beautiful sight, especially with the sun going down."

They hiked down, and Maggie was in awe. The beach and ocean looked rugged and untamed compared to her home coastline. She admired all of the spectacular rock formations that protruded from the Pacific.

She said, "Nature is an amazing sculptor, don't you think?"

"Just witness the crashing of the waves and the power of the wind. Let's walk further down and see if we can find a more sheltered spot that blocks the wind."

John located a protected area where they spread a large blanket on the sand. He got the wine out of the cooler and said, "I found this 2009 Siduri Pinot Noir and a wonderful local goat cheese."

"I love the label; it looks like something I would paint."

"She looks like you actually with your long auburn hair and full breasts. Siduri is the Babylonian Goddess of Wine."

"Perhaps I can depict her in one of my paintings?"

"We can take photographs of you in a vineyard."

"And you can perform a special wine tasting ritual."

John handed Maggie a glass of wine and said, "For now I would like to make a special toast. My dear Maggie O', I never want to offend you. My intentions are always meant to be in your best interest."

As they toasted Maggie said, "Please don't feel any guilt about what happened. I've replayed this morning and I was venting at the wrong person, my unfinished business in Chicago. You were truly brilliant in capturing those photos. I'm not sure I can artistically use them. They're so perfect in themselves. I feel like I would bastardize them in the process."

"Coach me on how you prefer to be photographed. I hate to say this, but I wish I could see the photos he took of you."

"That's the last thing I want to re-live."

"I'm sorry." John placed their wine glasses on top of the cooler and cupped her face in his hands. "Would you mind if I take some pictures of you here? I want to capture a profile of your body with the rocks being pounded by the waves and the sun as it starts to go down."

Maggie stripped naked and dropped to the blanket posing on her back with one knee up, and her hand buried between her loins. Unexpectedly, she had a flashback about her futile experience with Sean. She had given herself unconditionally to him. Given up her independent life to become his subordinate, his slave. He changed her in the process, showing her how pain heightened her pleasure in bed. She assumed the fetal position as she recalled how he enjoyed humiliating her, ejaculating all over her face, reminding her of how her own mother, Wanda had once punished her.

John stopped taking pictures. "What's wrong?"

Like a frightened child she embraced him. "Just hold me."

"Maggie O', you're shaking. Maybe we should leave."

"No kiss me."

He started comforting her with his kisses, sensually navigating her entire flesh. He buried himself between her creamy white thighs until she was totally satiated. He captured her afterglow on his Nikon.

Once she had recovered, Maggie stood up and watched the sunlight reflecting in the Pacific. Trance-like she walked to the edge of the water. When the sun started disappearing into the ocean, she knelt down towards it, letting go of her fragile past. The waves pounded against her pelvis extracting the toxins of her past and renewing her spirit.

She was oblivious that John was taking photos of her. Nor did she know how long it was before John helped her back on her feet. As the waves crashed around them, they started kissing with a level of passion she had never felt before.

"You must be freezing. Let me help you get dressed. It's getting late. We need to head back to the car."

John had brought two flashlights to help them find their way back in the dark. After he had opened the passenger car door, he undid his jeans and said, "This needs your immediate attention."

He sat down in the passenger seat, reclining the seat as far back as it would go. "Take off your jeans. Sit on top of me facing the windshield."

She quickly took off her jeans. Holding onto the dashboard, she lowered herself on him. John's hands lifted her shirt and teased her erect nipples. Balancing against the dashboard, she varied the angle she could penetrate him. The further she leaned forward, the greater the pressure on her G-spot. He grabbed right under her breasts and pulled her away from the dashboard. In this more upright position, he thrust even deeper. She moaned as he pushed against her cervix.

She heard his hoarse command, "Harder now."

She obeyed. She liked the power she had over him. When she sat straight up, his cock rammed against her cervix. He grunted like a wild animal as he released his spill.

Maggie fell asleep on the ride back. John woke her with a kiss on her cheek.

What time is it?"

"Almost 7:30."

"I still feel like I'm climaxing."

"You experienced a cervical orgasm. It's a full-body orgasm."

Maggie's feet were still sandy; she rinsed them off before filling up the tub.

John built a fire in the corner fireplace and brought in a bottle of champagne.

As she twisted her hair up, she said, "Why don't you get in the tub first so I can lean against you."

As they soaked in the warm, lavender scented water, he softly kissed her neck.

"John, you've never told me much about your family."

"My dad died at sixty of a heart attack; my mother passed away from a stroke two years ago."

"I'm sorry."

"They were quite the odd couple. Dad grew up in Manhattan and came from a conservative upper-class family. Mom grew up in Hoboken, New Jersey, living an impoverished life. She was sexually abused and abandoned by her father."

"How did your parents meet?"

"Mom was a stripper at a club in Atlantic City. My dad was attracted to her 36DDDD implants that a previous rich lover had given her for her twenty-first birthday. Shortly after she met my dad, she got pregnant with me."

"Do you think she trapped him?"

"When I turned eighteen, my dad sat me down, and we had our first beer drinking session together. After he'd had a few too many beers, he told me the truth and advised me never to let the need for sex control my life.

"Apparently my mom used sex as a weapon to get what she wanted. There were many nights she locked my dad out of their bedroom. She ended up leaving him when I was sixteen. She moved out of the house and went to live with her girlfriend, Ruby, who lived in Atlantic City. Ruby was thirty-one, eight years younger than Mom. She was gorgeous. It's uncanny how much you resemble her. Like my mother, Ruby turned tricks for a living.

"I went to visit them during my Christmas break. When I came back to the apartment early one night, I found my mother and Ruby having a threesome with a man on the rug in the living room. My mother's mouth was pressed between Ruby's spread legs, while the man was hammering my mother from behind. I became extremely aroused watching them."

"What happened then?"

"My mom told me to go to my room and several minutes later Ruby came to my room and started fondling my already hard cock. She placed the head in her mouth and sucked me, pulling away right before I came. She then told me goodnight, and I guess she went back to join my mother and her john. For the remainder of my Christmas vacation, Ruby taught me various ways to please a woman."

"Did you continue to see her after your Christmas vacation?"

"I was obsessed with her. Fortunately, right before I started college, her circumstances changed, and she moved on to Las Vegas. Now, tell me how you lost your virginity, I guess it has something to do the professor that painted you as a virgin."

"You have it all figured out. This bath water is getting cold; let's get out and order some oysters."

CHAPTER TEN

SIXTY PINK RIBBONS

Maggie had finished her second cup of coffee when John came in ready to leave for work. "Sorry I can't take you to the train station; I'm meeting with a new client."

"That's fine. We will see each other Friday."

"I hate asking you this, but what are your plans after then?"

"I'm going back on Sunday. I need to spend some time at home before I return to New York. Matthew has scheduled a ski vacation over Valentine's Day. I'll be filling in for him at the gallery. When I get back from New York, would you like to come see me at the beach?"

"I'll look at my schedule. I might be able to come see you towards the end of February."

Sharon had driven to the Caltrain station in Palo Alto to pick up Maggie. "How about we get some lunch before we head over?"

"Could we go somewhere for a burger? I'm dying for something unhealthy. You know how Mr. Control carefully plans every meal I eat."

"There's a Kirk's Steakburgers just up the road. How is your relationship with Mr. Control going?"

"He is like a stallion in bed."

"Please be careful; don't get bucked off again."

"I'm trying not to get my hopes up this time."

"Is there more to it than sex?"

"I can't tell right now."

"Who knows, you may have finally met the perfect mate."

"Isn't 'perfect mate' an oxymoron?"

"Let's go inside to eat."

In the restroom, Maggie confessed, "Mary tells me I need to play hard to get, that I'm too available."

"Are you?"

Maggie retrieved her cell phone from her purse. "I just remembered I need to text him and let him know I arrived. He just sent a text asking why I haven't texted him."

Sharon shook her head in disapproval. "He does have you on a short leash. Ignore it until after we eat. Let's order our lunch."

Maggie ordered the patty melt and steak fries, while Sharon, a strict vegetarian, ordered a green salad and sweet potato fries.

"I hope I'm not grossing you out eating this burger? Now I want to hear about your new boyfriend, Mark."

"I'll tell you about him at happy hour tonight. We need to finish lunch, head over to the clinic and get started."

Back in the car Maggie responded to John's text.

"Just finished lunch and heading to the clinic."

"I'm missing you already. When you're alone tonight, call me."

"I won't be alone. Sharon and I are sharing a room."

The new wing of the clinic had a large focal wall perfect for displaying the paintings. Sharon and Maggie had already designed a grid of where each piece would hang. At the end of the day, they had hung twenty canvases. They expected to be finished with the remaining forty canvases by early afternoon the next day.

The clinic provided two maintenance workers to assist them. Luis and Miguel were attractive Hispanic brothers in their mid-to-late twenties. They enjoyed flirting with Sharon and Maggie and wanted the women to meet them for happy hour at a Mexican restaurant that their cousin owned. Maggie overheard them talking in Spanish how they wanted to pair up. Miguel, the younger brother, wanted the Southern redhead with the big melons. Luis liked the blonde with the shapely bottom. Maggie surprised them when she spoke fluently back to them in Spanish that they already had plans for the evening.

Maggie had reserved a deluxe room with two queen beds at the Stanford Park Hotel. A petite blonde clerk handed Maggie three room access cards. She told Maggie, "These two cards are for your room on the first floor. This keycard is for a second room on the third floor. Your boss called in and reserved this room. He requested I give you his card."

Maggie turned to Sharon, "You go ahead to our room. I'll join you after I check out the boss's room."

Maggie climbed the stairs to the third floor. She unlocked the door and found an inviting over-sized room with a gas-burning fireplace. On the coffee table, there was a bottle of champagne in an ice bucket. She read the note next to it, *"Please warm up this bed for me. Can't wait to see you Friday."*

Maggie called down to the front desk and asked them to deliver her luggage to John's room.

She texted John, *"What a pleasant surprise, thank you. I only wish you were here."*

He immediately texted back, *"If it weren't for Sharon being there, I would be. I wouldn't want to get in the way of your girl time together."*

"I'll text you when I'm alone. Do you realize that we've been together more days recently than we've been apart?"

"Sorry, I don't want to be late for a dinner appointment. I have to leave now."

101

She called Sharon and invited her to have champagne. At six, Sharon knocked on the door. Maggie opened the door wearing her yoga pants and a thin tank top, which she wore braless. Sharon was similarly attired; except she wore a special mastectomy sports bra.

Maggie had already opened the champagne and poured each of them a glass. She had also ordered several appetizers.

Sharon said, "Wow, your controlling boyfriend thinks of everything."

"Why would you say that?"

"He has put you in this beautiful birdcage until he can be with you."

Sharon's remark hurt Maggie. In his defense, she responded, "He's actually generous!"

Sharon said, "That's one way to look at it. I've no business giving you love advice. I brought some pot. Would you like some?"

"Sure. Let me turn the gas logs in the fireplace on. It will cover up the pot smell."

"Mark wants to see me tonight. Do you mind? He's been out of town all week on a business trip."

"Why would I mind?" Looking forward to calling John later, she said, "Besides, I want to get to bed early tonight."

Sharon handed Maggie the joint. The last time she had smoked pot was during her fall visit to Sharon's. After only three hits, she was high. She coughed as she exhaled the smoke. "Tell me about Mark."

"Our relationship is still in an awkward stage."

"How's that?"

"The one time we had sex, I kept my shirt on and the lights were out. He hasn't seen my battle scars yet. I suspect my having had a radical mastectomy scares him. I probably should have taken the risk and had a modified mastectomy instead."

"But your tumor was growing into the pectoral muscle. You made the right choice."

Maggie took Sharon's hand and squeezed it. "Sharon, you're the most beautiful person I know. Always remember that."

Sharon had taken two last hits while Mark waited for her in the lobby.

"You're sure you don't want to meet him now?"

"Have a great time tonight; I'll be okay here. Give me a hug before you leave. See you in the morning."

There was a little bit of champagne left which Maggie finished. Her senses were overloaded; everything was more beautiful and bright. Sharon always had the most amazing pot. Maggie wondered how John would be if he were high; would he let his guard down? She texted him that she could talk now.

He immediately called her. When he found out that Sharon was with her boyfriend he asked Maggie, "Would you mind if I see you tomorrow? I can get to your hotel by late afternoon."

"That would be won-der-ful."

"Maggie, you sound tipsy."

"A little. I'm horny right now."

"Why don't you get Buzz out and play with him while I tell you a naughty bedtime story."

Maggie woke up excited that she would see John in the afternoon. Her mood changed when she read his earlier text message. *"I just realized I have an important partner's dinner this evening and have to cancel seeing you tonight. Call me when you're awake."*

Deflated by his change of plans, in haste, she texted him back, *"Don't bother coming to the opening exhibit. I'll be too busy that night. Also Sharon has invited me to spend a few days with her before I head back to Gulf Shores."*

After they finished hanging all the paintings, Maggie said, "I want to pass on going out to dinner with you and Mark tonight and get to bed early. How did last night go with Mark?"

"He got fairly drunk and couldn't stay erect. I ended up giving him a blowjob. He apologized this morning and said he would make it up to me tonight."

Maggie ordered a half-bottle of Chardonnay and burger and fries from room service. At Sharon's suggestion, Maggie ignored her phone for the next three hours. Maggie felt like she was having withdrawal symptoms. At nine, she heard yet another ping on her phone. She could no longer resist the temptation. Retrieving her phone from her purse, she saw numerous texts, all from John asking her to call or text him back. As tempting as it was, she did not text him back. *Why had she let another man control her like this?* She finished her wine, turned off her phone, and went to bed at ten.

Just after midnight, Maggie was awakened by a knock. She hurriedly put on her robe, walked over to the door, and said, "Who is it?"

"Maggie, it's me, can I come in?"

When Maggie opened the door she found Sharon in tears. She had never seen Sharon cry before. "Come in; what happened?"

"Mark told me he needed to move on. That he didn't have what it takes to have an intimate relationship with me. He made me feel like I was a freak."

Maggie embraced Sharon and said, "He doesn't have the balls. What a prick he is. He doesn't deserve you."

Maggie leaned forward and pressed her mouth against Sharon's cheek. "Stay with me tonight. Sit on the bed."

Maggie helped Sharon remove her ankle boots and blue jeans. Sharon stripped down to her bra and bikini panties and slipped under the bedcovers, resting on her side.

Maggie turned on the gas logs and switched off the bedside lamp. The room had a soft amber glow. Dropping her robe, she hesitated before she snuggled naked behind Sharon, holding her in the spooning position.

Between her sobs, Sharon said, "Maggie, I love you. You're such a good friend."

Maggie was overcome with this amazing protective bond she felt. "I love you too."

"Do you remember when we were in our hotel room in Puerto Vallarta, trying out the new vibrators we'd bought in San Francisco?"

Maggie added, "How could I forget that night? We'd had way too much tequila."

"I have a confession. I got turned on watching you that night."

After several silent minutes, Maggie removed Sharon's bra and said, "Roll over on your back."

Maggie straddled Sharon's petite frame. She gazed into her friend's tear-filled eyes and tenderly brushed Sharon's tears away. Maggie asked, "What stopped you?"

"I was afraid of how you would react."

Sharon put her arms around Maggie's neck and ran her slender fingers through Maggie's hair. She drew Maggie towards her, their lips barely touched. Maggie lightly kissed Sharon's scar and hungrily moved to her dearest friend's lush mouth. Maggie had never experienced a kiss so tender and giving. It felt natural for her to slide her hand underneath Sharon's panties, pulling them down. For the first time, she intimately touched another woman. She softly stroked her, causing Sharon to moan and raise her hips. Within several precious minutes, Sharon released herself.

Sharon said, "Now, let me take care of you."

"No, Sweetie. I want this to be all about you."

Maggie woke up to discover a note on the bedside table.

Maggie,

You're the most wonderful friend I've ever had. I will always remember how you comforted me last night.

Love, Sharon

Some things change you forever. Sharon and Maggie would never again speak about what happened that night.

Sharon said, "Maggie, you've hardly touched your lunch. Why are you letting this guy get to you like this?"

"Can't I find someone who isn't controlling and be happy at the same time?"

"You just came off a two-year sabbatical and you're like a bitch in heat."

Maggie sighed, "I know. I've got to stop acting this way."

"Do you love this guy?"

"I don't know if I love him or if I just desperately want to be in love again."

The reception started at 6 p.m. and Maggie was happy to see that Sharon and her paintings had captivated the guests. One of the clinic's partners insisted on keeping Maggie company. He quickly let her know he had been divorced for two years. Extremely attractive, he reminded her of McDreamy on the TV show, Grey's Anatomy.

Maggie was not answering John's phone calls or texts. He questioned whether he should show up; she'd either be surprised or angry.

When he arrived at seven, he spotted Maggie wearing a plunging neckline pink raw silk suit and a Mikimoto pearl choker that drew full attention to her décolletage. He was annoyed when he realized she was talking to an attractive man, grabbed two glasses of champagne, and made his surprise attack. Ambushing Maggie, he offered her a glass of champagne, then put his arm around her waist. The bewildered doctor excused himself.

John said, "Your seductive marketing skills amaze me."

"Excuse me, you're the expert at seduction."

"You were obviously leading that guy on, wearing such a provocative outfit."

"Dr. Andrews is one of the partners at the clinic; I most definitely wasn't leading him on. Jealousy doesn't become you."

"I'm not jealous. I just happen to be real observant."

"More like intrusive."

"I give in, Maggie O'. It's time for make-up sex, don't you agree?"

After a polite time at the reception, they headed for the hotel room. Maggie noticed that John had straightened the bedcovers and prepared the bed with the restraints. Turning her back to John, she undid her conservative French twist and used her fingers to comb her unruly auburn hair. She unbuttoned her jacket and cupped her breasts lifting them slightly. Shrugging her shoulders back, she removed her jacket, letting it fall to the floor.

John gazed at her sensual back. He had been right, she was braless under her jacket. He admired how her tight pencil skirt accentuated her small waist and well-rounded bottom. Her arms reached behind her as she unbuttoned the skirt and slid the zipper down, allowing the silk to puddle on the floor. She turned around and stepped over it facing him. All that remained on was her pearl choker, nude thigh high-hose, and five-inch taupe stilettos. Maggie teased John as she touched her sensitive nipples.

"Stop touching yourself. I know what you're doing. You're trying to keep me distracted so I won't discipline you. You have several serious infractions."

"And why am I being disciplined?"

"Don't be so coy. First of all, you didn't let me know when you arrived in Palo Alto. Tonight, I caught you flirting with that doctor. It's obvious that you smoked pot in this room. Oh, I found a receipt from Kirk's Steakburger. How were the burger and fries?"

Maggie started laughing. "Honestly, John, is that the best you can come up with? I'm truly disappointed in you. Did you not have the sheets on the bed analyzed for traces of the DNA left by the men I've been sleeping with?"

John pulled out Sharon's panties from under the sheets. "I know you're more the thong type. Should I have the DNA on these analyzed?"

There was a minute of silence between them. John sat down on edge of the bed. "Imagining you with a woman has aroused me."

Maggie kneeled in front of John and removed his trousers.

CHAPTER ELEVEN

SUMMER OF 2001

While waiting at the Atlanta Airport for her connecting flight to Pensacola, Maggie discovered an email from Chris.

"I was in New York on business and I stopped by The Launch, hoping to find you there. I've so much I want to say to you. A day doesn't go by that I don't think about you. I still love you, Maggie"

It was after 10 p.m. when she got home. Even though the temperature had dropped below fifty degrees, she opened all of the windows, wanting the bad demons from the summer of 2001 to fly away.

When Chris returned to the beach cottage that summer, he had an even stronger physical attraction to eighteen-year-old Maggie. It amazed him how much she had changed in the three years since he had last seen her. *What a beaut she had become.* She looked and acted much older than her age. He wondered if she was still a virgin.

Several days after Chris arrived, Wanda used the excuse to go out. She had a meeting with Maggie's executor, Ross Johnson. Bessie had gone to the grocery store leaving them all alone. Maggie put on her new lavender string bikini and walked into Chris's bedroom where he was working on his short story collection. Walking over to him, she untied her top, dropping it on the floor. Chris stood up, and Maggie pressed her mouth to

109

his. He could not resist her as he kissed her and fondled her breasts. Maggie grabbed Chris's hand and guided it underneath her bikini bottom; he started stroking her.

In anguish, he moaned, "Maggie, we must not do this."

"Why not? I want you to take my virginity. I've saved myself for you. I've never allowed any other guy to touch me. Nor have I touched a guy before. Please be my lover. Teach me what I need to know."

That summer Chris became an attentive teacher. He taught Maggie the pleasures of her body. She remembered the day he slid his two fingers inside her and how she finally sensed what it must feel like to be taken. His touch felt different from when she stroked herself.

Maggie soon started exploring Chris. While initially she was content with pleasing him orally, she later begged him that she wanted to go all the way.

"Maggie, it's much too risky. You aren't on birth control." He explained that there was an alternative, but he would need to gradually get her ready.

One night, Maggie woke up hearing a loud sound thinking it was another summer thunderstorm. But the noise was not thunder; it resonated from upstairs. Maggie tiptoed down the hall past Bessie's room and quietly climbed the wooden stairs. She wanted to pay Chris a visit, but knew that would be too risky. The sound was coming from her mother's room. The door was slightly open to allow the air to circulate. Somewhat drowned out by the hum of the ceiling fan, Maggie listened as her mother begged, "Make me come now." Maggie looked through the door crack and saw her mother lying naked on her stomach, blindfolded, and tied spread eagle to her four-poster bed. Naked Chris stood next to the bed holding what looked like a riding crop. Maggie's heart started racing as she realized she better go back to her room before they discovered her spying.

In her room, she was trying to sort out what she had just witnessed. She was jealous seeing Chris with her mother. It surprised her to see her *always in control* mother allowing someone to tie her up in such a bizarre fashion.

The next afternoon as Chris and she swam in the Gulf, Maggie told him how she had spied on them.

"Why does Mother do such an odd thing?"

Chris wasn't sure what to say. Wanda had recently introduced him to her fetish need to be dominated. At first it aroused Chris, tying up Wanda and marking her flesh with a crop. One day, he noticed that she had fresh marks on her chest that he had not made. Wanda confessed to him about her affair with Ross. She suggested that the three of them get together and that Ross was into kink and might enjoy Chris's tight ass.

Chris said, "Some women enjoy being dominated during sex."

"What was the riding crop for?"

He waited before answering, "Some people are sexually aroused by pain."

"That's bizarre. Will you let me see if I would like that?"

Under the water, he squeezed Maggie's bottom. "No, you would end up with red marks on your fair skinned bottom."

Maggie didn't like his response. She slipped her hand inside his swim shorts and squeezed him. "I don't like it when you don't let me experience all these things you do with Mother."

"When you go off to college and are on the pill, I'll allow you any pleasure you desire, that is, if you still want me."

"Of course. I'll want you. I want to marry you one day."

"I'm too old for you. Now stop groping me like that; I'm starting to get a hard-on."

"I know how to take care of that. Let's walk down the beach to our special spot."

The next day Bessie left to visit her family for the weekend in Birmingham. Wanda went out with Kim to celebrate her forty-fifth birthday at the Flora-Bama, a popular nightspot on the Alabama Florida state line. Wanda told Maggie she would be spending the night at Kim's Ono Island house.

For the first night, Chris and Maggie were alone. Maggie imagined she was on her first date. She lit the lavender scented pillar candle that sat on the coffee table, and Chris turned on a soft jazz station. Maggie had heated a frozen pizza for their dinner. Chris allowed her a small glass of Australian wine he had bought.

After dinner, they took a beach blanket down next to the water. Maggie leaned against Chris's muscular chest, and he tenderly held her close, and she knew she had fallen in love with her prince.

As the sun faded into the horizon, they came back inside. Chris suggested they go upstairs to his room. This was a big step for them both. Chris played Elton John's *Something About The Way You Look Tonight* on his CD player.

"Maggie, tonight is special. Come here."

Maggie wore a white gauze sundress that tied behind her neck and her Victoria Secret white lace bikini panties. She had tied a lavender scarf around her low ponytail. Chris untied her scarf and threw it aside, releasing her long wavy auburn hair. The summer sun had brought out her freckles.

"You're a beautiful young woman. When you go to college, you're going to meet so many guys who will want you. Are you sure you want to still do this?"

"You know I do. I love you."

"I love you too."

112

She untied her dress, and Chris pulled it over her head. Scooping her up, he carried her to his bed. Removing his rugby shorts freed his fully erect cock, which Maggie had nicknamed, her "sea serpent." He took off her white lace panties.

She felt Chris's two familiar greased fingers inside her tight anus. He had been training her on how to relax to lessen the pain as he penetrated her. He reminded her to take slow, deep breaths. He removed his fingers and held her hips steady while he slowly inched inside her. While at first it was painful, the longer he stayed inside, the less it hurt.

"Are you still okay? I'm almost all the way in. Just try and relax."

"Yes. I want all of you."

Chris moved slowly in and out, and Maggie could not stop moaning. As he got harder and faster, his moans got louder than hers.

He groaned, "I can't hold back."

Maggie was overcome with joy that she could give him this pleasure. She believed this would always be the most wonderful day of her life as she fell asleep in his arms.

Early the next morning, Chris woke her up. "We better get up before your mother comes home. I need to shower, and so do you. Would you like to go for an early walk after we shower?"

"I've other ideas of what I would like to do with that sea serpent of yours that filled me with that deadly poison last night, but I guess a walk will have to do."

Chris tenderly kissed her forehead and said, "You're becoming such a tease, Maggie."

"I can't wait until you take me the other way."

"Be patient; it won't be much longer."

When they returned from their walk, they found Wanda smoking a Capri cigarette and drinking a Bloody Mary. Her car was not outside, and she still wore her black halter dress from the night before. Her war paint was smeared. The way she slurred her words, they could tell she was still intoxicated.

Wanda said, "Well, how are you lovebirds doing today?"

Caught off guard, Maggie couldn't think of what to say. "Mother, where is your car?"

"Someone brought me here and just in time. Maggie, dear you're not good at covering your tracks. I can tell that your bed wasn't slept in, and Chris your bed looks like you hosted a slumber party. I found Maggie's lavender scarf on the floor next to the footboard.

"You both disgust me, doing this behind my back. I'm tempted to expose what you've done to your family, Chris. I would hate to see your trust fund cut off. However, I have another idea for your punishment. Unless you want me to call your father?"

"But...Maggie is still a virgin. I promise we've never had intercourse."

"You expect me to believe you, Chris. Both of you come upstairs with me. Maggie, how dare you do this to me. You inherited my parent's entire estate so that I'm penniless on my own. And now you've whored around with Chris. What more do you want to take from me? I want you to watch me as I punish Chris and see how it feels to be betrayed."

Upstairs Wanda untied her dress, dropping it on her bedroom floor. Underneath the dress, she wore a black brocade corset and a black satin garter belt with matching bikini panties and black fishnet hose.

When Maggie was a child, she would sneak into her mother's room and examine her mother's lingerie chest. Maggie didn't know that Ross Johnson was overbilling her estate so he could buy Wanda this expensive French lingerie along with all the BDSM items she'd locked away in her Grandmother Mona's cedar hope chest. Wanda conveniently kept the chest at the foot of the bed. Maggie had several times tried to pick the lock but was unsuccessful.

Wanda took a key out of her bedside drawer and unlocked the chest. She pulled out the riding crop and said, "I'm surprised Chris hasn't done that to you before. Now slave brace yourself."

Maggie cried, "No. Punish me instead."

"Be quiet, or I'll make it worse on him."

Maggie silently counted the number of times her mother whacked Chris. When she stopped after twenty-seven times, there was hardly an area on his buttocks left unmarked.

Wanda said, "Maggie, my blowjobs keep men coming back. Come kneel by me and watch how quickly I can arouse Chris."

Maggie was disgusted watching her mother deep throat Chris; something that Maggie was still having difficulty doing. She could tell by his moans that he was about to come. Her mother switched over to a hand job and she directed his cum so that it squirted all over Maggie's face and hair. Maggie felt degraded. Sobbing, she tried wiping herself off with the bottom of her tank top.

Wanda said to Chris, "Pack your stuff and get out of here before noon."

That night, Maggie took her grandfather's pocketknife out and pierced her finger. As she looked at the oozing blood, she said, "I'll never forgive you, Mother."

CHAPTER TWELVE

LIFE AND GUMBO

She poured a glass of Hennessy Cognac into a Waterford brandy snifter, a remnant of her dismal marriage. As a 'Society Worthy Southern Bride', she was blessed with a complete formal dinner service for twelve. While she continued to use the Waterford Crystal, the Wedgewood fine china and Wallace sterling silver flatware were still packed away in their original boxes. For some reason, she couldn't let go of these wedding gifts from her past.

As she walked outside on the screened porch, she tuned in to the familiar song of the waves breaking against the beach. The sound was ingrained in her soul; she was drawn into the darkest memories of her past.

The only light was a waxing crescent moon. The cognac had not helped disguise her emptiness. As she walked back inside the cottage, she thought, *Perhaps, I was better off living a celibate life.*

Pouring a second glass of cognac, she remembered the sensation of watching the Stranger undress her with his eyes. Her crotch ached just thinking about him.

She downloaded her favorite video, Sade's *No Ordinary Love*. Its lyrics and mermaid graphics always brought back memories of those summers with Chris.

Maggie slept under her favorite lavender down comforter until daybreak. When she woke up, the temperature had dropped to the low forties. Closing all the windows, she turned on the heater and put on her warmest sweats. The cognac had left a cloud in her brain. She needed coffee before she could respond to Chris's unexpected email.

As she sipped her coffee, she read it once again. His email brought back the pain she had felt when her mother had told her he had married someone. She looked at the faint scars down her forearm and remembered the day she first cut herself and how self-injury had numbed the emotional pain his leaving had caused her. She retrieved her grandfather's bone handled pocketknife from her jewelry box, opened its sharp blade, and cut herself before she emailed him back.

"I will contact you when I'm ready to talk. Don't you realize how much you hurt me?"

She watched the blood running down her arm as she hit the send key. Having never stopped loving Chris, she had only adapted to the reality of the situation. She had given Chris a part of her heart no other man would ever share.

Maggie climbed the narrow stairs rising to her studio loft. When she reached the top of the landing, she stared at the large empty canvas that Matthew had previously given her as an enticement for her to start painting again.

Her phoned pinged; she had a message from John. Her mood shifted as she read his message.

"Beautiful Maggie O' Hopefully you're home and resting. I'm already missing you. Let's talk later."

"I'm missing you as well. I think I'm motivated to start painting again."

She had created a playlist that included songs by her favorite female vocalists: Sade, Mariah Carey, Carol King, and Beyoncé. She walked over to her CD player, pushed play, and Beyoncé's version of *Sex on Fire* started.

117

Several hours later, she noticed another text from John, *"Wonderful. I'm so glad you're inspired."*

During the next ten days, Maggie transformed the empty canvas into a masterpiece she titled *Metamorphosis*. She painted three different timelines on the large horizontal canvas. In the first scene, a nude Maggie was sitting on a rock formation that overlooked the Pacific in the fog during a violent thunderstorm. Her face was partially hidden as she stared out at the ocean. Her taut, full breasts were the focal point. Drawn back into the dark days of her past, it was the most difficult self-portrait Maggie had ever done.

The second scene captured her with a sensual glow after John brought her back into the present. The storm had passed, and she was nude lying on her back on a red blanket as the sun was starting to set. The third scene was her rite of passage. As the sun disappeared into the Pacific, Maggie was kneeling down at the edge of the water, letting go of the demons of her past and returning to the innocence of her youth. Her auburn hair was held back in a ponytail by the lavender scarf she had kept from thirteen years ago.

It was Wednesday, February fifth, and Maggie began packing for her New York trip. Matthew and his latest lover, Joseph, were going on a trip to Steamboat, Colorado with Ski Bums LGBT skiing and snowboarding club. Maggie would be in charge of the gallery in his absence. Going back to the Big Apple would seem lonely without John's company. She sent John a text.

"Wish you could be in New York while I'm there."

"Fortunately, I'll see you on the twenty-second. Where are you staying?"

"At Matthew's."

"You're welcome to stay at my place."
"Thanks, but I'm taking care of his cat."
"I'd like to take care of your cat."
"Meow . . ."

Being inside Matthew's apartment brought back memories of her and Matthew as playful lovers. Her phone pinged; she saw John's text.

"Make sure you let me know when you arrive."

Matthew's cat rubbed against her legs. Guido was unusually affectionate. She stroked him before texting John back.

"You know, you can be like a mother hen sometimes. No delays. Unfortunately… I didn't get to meet a stranger in the airport this time."

"I'll call you later. I'm in a meeting."

Maggie found a note on the coffee table next to a heart shaped box of chocolates. She read the note aloud.

"Please make yourself at home. I got you some pastrami, corned beef, and rye bread from Katz's Deli. Happy Early Valentine's Day. Love xoxoxo Matthew."

Maggie had not even recalled it being close to Valentine's Day. *Why do I find myself in these impossible relationships? There's no shortage of men to mess around with, but I'm ready for more. I want what I thought I had with Sean before he lied to me. Or what Chris and I once had before he broke his promise to me. Now I'm falling for a charming, controlling, commitment phobic, borderline narcissist.*

Saturday was a productive day at the gallery. Maggie sold one of Frank's small metal sculptures for $1,250 and a large painting by another new artist from Rome, Georgia for $1,950. She called both artists to tell them the good news. Maggie asked Connie to run to Maman and bring back quiche and their famous nutty chocolate chunk cookies for their lunch. She checked her messages, and John had texted, *"Maggie O', only two more weeks."*

It was Friday, February 14. Connie's fiancé had sent her a dozen red roses. The only time Maggie had been given flowers was when Chris had sent her sixteen purple tulips for her sixteenth birthday.

Just before four, Maggie was working in her office when Connie came in and said, "There's an artist outside who was supposed to meet with Matthew today."

Maggie looked at Matthew's appointment calendar. "I guess Matthew forgot to write down the appointment."

Maggie walked out to the gallery and was surprised to see John holding a Jiannetto's pizza box. Her heart raced as she walked over to hug him. She said, "You like to surprise me don't you?"

"Peek inside the box."

She opened the pizza box and saw a heart-shaped pepperoni pizza.

"Yum. How sweet."

"I didn't want you to spend Valentine's Day by yourself."

Teasing John, she said, "You're rather presumptuous."

"I must admit, I am."

"Are you planning on spending the night?"

"I'm taking Amtrak to Philadelphia tomorrow morning."

"You have an appointment on a Saturday?"

"That's how everyone's schedule worked out."

"I'll have Connie lock up. I'll be back in a minute."

They took a taxi to Matthew's to check on Guido, and she hurriedly packed an overnight bag. She was thrilled that John was with her, if only for one night.

As they rode up to the thirty-ninth floor, John took the pizza box from Maggie and placed it on the floor. He pressed her against the elevator wall and kissed her. Her pelvis welcomed his hardness. She moaned, "I like how you distract me from my acrophobia."

Once inside his condo, the pizza was put in the refrigerator, and they quickly convened to the master bedroom.

She had worn an emerald green cashmere tunic over her black leggings and her thigh high black leather Jimmy Choo boots. As John helped her take her boots off, he said, "I'm surprised you're dressed rather conservatively."

"Had I known I had an appointment today, I would have worn something more provocative."

John finished undressing her and said, "What happened to your arm. Did you cut yourself?"

"Believe or not, Guido scratched me. Matthew refuses to get him declawed. Now let me unzip your trousers. Let's make the most of our short time together."

No props were needed after eighteen days without any direct physical contact. Maggie could not get enough of John as every imaginable sex position was tried and a few new ones invented.

At four in the morning, John jokingly said to her, "Damn, Maggie O', I never imagined anyone could last as long as we just did."

After spending eleven days in New York, Maggie was happy to be back home again. The day before John's arrival, Maggie wrote a story for him to read on his trip. It was based on an erotic fantasy she often had but had never told anyone about. She spent most of the day completing it. At 10 p.m., she sent it to him and immediately had second thoughts about what she had done.

On his flight, John was enthralled as he read her sadomasochist story. He wondered if she was suggesting he assume the role of the Professor and discipline her.

Maggie was once again at the Pensacola Airport. John's United Airlines flight was scheduled to arrive at 2:23 a.m. She found John already waiting for her in the baggage claim area. Sneaking up behind him, she said, "Howdy, stranger. Would you like some help with your luggage?"

John turned around, immediately kissed her, then whacked her bottom and said, "I liked your story."

As they drove along the lower Alabama coast, Maggie said, "When I was a little girl, many of these high-rise condos had not yet been built. You could still see the sugar white sand and the beautiful Gulf of Mexico. There are too many high-rises blocking the view now. We call these high-density areas ant hills; there's too much money being made at the expense of the environment."

John said, "I imagine this area is probably the largest tax revenue generator for the state."

"Probably, although we haven't totally recovered from the BP oil spill. These beaches have seen more than enough hurricanes these last several years. While hurricanes are destructive, they are part of our eco-system, and new life is created as a by-product. But with the oil spill disaster, our coastal environment has been compromised and impaired.

"You must be hungry. There are several places we could stop." Her eyes diverted to him as she said, "I also have food at my place."

John's left hand rested on Maggie's right upper thigh. He made his way under her skirt to her bare crotch.

"After reading your story, I've only one thing on my mind."

"You need to stop distracting me. Want to go straight to my place?"

"You're sinfully wet right now. Maybe we should pull over."

"We're almost there. Can't you put your cock in mute mode for now?"

Maggie turned into a crushed shelled driveway marked with a whimsical sign she had painted, *Mermaid's Grotto*. John said, "I could find your place just by the sign in front of it. The mermaid looks exactly like you."

She parked her Tahoe between the pilings that elevated the lavender painted cottage. They walked up the steep stairs to the main level; as Maggie turned the key, John fondled her.

"I guess you want to see my bedroom first."

Maggie led John to her grotto bedroom; they immediately got reacquainted and came up for air two hours later.

"I've never had sex in a grotto before."

"I guess I went a little overboard. I've a friend who builds movie sets. He helped me design and construct it."

"Obviously you painted all the underwater murals; even though you weren't painting on canvases, you were still painting."

"I guess I was. I escaped in my imaginary mermaid world."

"And that beautiful mermaid on the wall is a self-portrait."

"I've a knack for painting myself; I'm somewhat narcissistic."

"I think it's amazing how realistic you paint yourself with no enhancements."

"When I have to do enhancements, I'll no longer do self-portraits. I know it seems silly, almost Disneyworld like."

"I don't think it's silly. I think it's erotic--certainly not *Little Mermaid*."

"You're the first man to have been with me in my grotto."

"I'm honored."

Maggie showed John the rest of the main level before pouring some wine. "Let's take our wine out on the screened porch and watch the sunset."

John said, "I love your place here. Did you have it built?"

"The original place was built by my grandparents right after Hurricane Frederick in 1980. Its footprint was twice as large, but it wasn't elevated high enough to escape the surge. It was completely destroyed during Hurricane Ivan. I couldn't decide if I wanted to sell the beachfront lot or rebuild."

"I like how you've not wasted any space and incorporated the outside into your living space."

"When it's warmer, I often sleep on the porch, hearing the crashing waves and breathing the salt air."

"Where do you paint?"

"In the loft."

"I want to see the painting you just completed."

Upstairs, Maggie turned on a spotlight to illuminate the large painting. John was mesmerized by her meticulous attention to details and by its emotional impact.

He said, "It's fascinating the way you merged my photos into this erotic story you've painted."

"It's the most complicated painting I've ever done."

John embraced her and said, "I can only imagine. You have incredible talent."

Downstairs they refilled their wine glasses. Maggie said, "We can go out for dinner or eat in. I have gumbo and French bread here."

"I haven't had gumbo since I was in New Orleans. Let's stay in."

While Maggie was heating up the gumbo and bread, John looked at her limited wine supply and said, "I see you have several bottles of Skinny Bitch and this bottle of Cougar Juice."

"The Rombauer Chardonnay was given to me by Matthew when I turned thirty."

"Do you mind if we go wine shopping tomorrow? I'll buy you another bottle of Cougar Juice to replace this one. That gumbo smells good."

"When I was growing up, I used to watch our housekeeper, Bessie, make gumbo. She made quite a production of it. She would tell me how life and gumbo were so much alike. She said, "Maggie, dear, just like when making a roux you must exercise patience so you don't get burned. And just like in life you should never leave out the holy trinity.""

"Chef Paul Prudhomme popularized that phrase."

"Yes, it refers to the celery, onion, and bell pepper used in Cajun and Creole dishes. Bessie and I used to watch his TV cooking show."

As Maggie ladled the gumbo into two bowls, she said, "I remember Bessie telling me, "No two gumbos are alike, just like no two people are alike. So don't get upset when someone doesn't care for your recipe. You'll eventually find someone who does.""

They sat down at a round table tucked into the large bay window, which perfectly framed the view of the Gulf. John said, "Marvelous view. What an interesting table. Did you paint the mermaid?"

"As a side business, I produce custom painted furniture and upholstery for an interior designer friend. I rescued the table from a flea market."

"Did you make the chandelier?"

"I found a discarded brass chandelier at the Humanity Restore, painted it sea foam green and added the sea glass and shells. When I was rebuilding, I tried to use recycled building materials whenever I could. I'm also totally off the grid with solar panels."

"It looks great how you put it all together. I remember following the hurricane on the news."

"I had just started my senior year at Alabama. When I came back after the storm, the house was completely gone. The only thing remaining was this bronze mermaid statue now sitting on the coffee table. I was surprised when I discovered it; mother had told me she had gotten rid of it."

"She's exquisite."

"When I was a teen, someone had their friend who was a sculptor make her for me."

"She looks like you."

Maggie glanced at the bronze statue. *How innocent and vulnerable I once was.*

CHAPTER THIRTEEN

MERMAIDS

As John helped Maggie put away the leftovers, he said, "It's interesting how you obviously like mermaids. Do you know how the myth may have started?"

"I don't, but I'm sure you do."

"Apparently, the vagina of a female manatee is of similar construction to that of a human female. To cover up their acts of bestiality, sailors claimed they'd had intercourse with a mermaid."

"That's just sick."

"Manatees are referred to as 'pirate's pussy."

At 3 a.m., Maggie rolled over to find John sound asleep. Wide-awake, she got out of bed and went to the loft. Fiddling with her CD player, she located Sade's *The Sweetest Taboo* and painted with abandonment. It amazed her how sex, painting, and music were interconnected for her. During her last visit to Ron's, he'd told her, "Before you learned that, you were just an above-average art major. You're the type of artist who must experience passion in your life to express it in your paintings."

Effortlessly, she painted John as a pirate taking her as a mermaid from behind. Just outside the grotto, next to the shore, there were two other mermaids with their wrists tied together preventing them from swimming away from the pirate.

She finished the entire painting just before dawn, signed it, "Maggie O', and fell asleep exhausted on her loft bed. Around

10 a.m., she woke with John's cock pressed against her backside. As she rolled over to face him, she teasingly said, "Do I know you?"

"Good morning. The Grotto got lonely. I hope you don't mind me sleeping with you in your loft?"

"I'm sorry I abandoned you last night."

"Looks like you were inspired. Your new painting is extremely moving, but I'm having trouble with its hidden meaning."

"What do you mean?"

"I see a pirate who resembles me. He is exploiting the mermaids. Do you think I'm like a pirate?"

"Are you?"

"In my profession, that would be somewhat of a satire, one could argue."

"But in the sexual sense, would you like to be the pirate?"

"Only in the fantasy sense, not at the expense of our relationship."

It was a beautiful late morning, not as chilly as the previous day, but the beach was just as deserted. Maggie and John completed three miles of their run and then walked the last mile.

"Maggie, I'm curious about the professor story you wrote. Was that the type of relationship you had with Ron?"

"Sort of."

"How about your relationship with Sean?"

Maggie hesitated for a moment. "Sometimes, before Sean would allow me to climax, he made me beg to be flogged. Oddly my best artwork was produced then; being his submissive somehow stimulated my creativity."

"That's not unusual. Van Gogh did what many considered his best work when he committed himself to an asylum."

"I didn't realize you knew so much art history?"

"I took a class summer semester in college. Did you enjoy being Sean's submissive?"

"At first I did. But then he went past my limits."

"So he became more abusive."

"My life was so screwed up then."

"You told me previously that he enjoyed erotic asphyxiation."

"He never did it alone, however, I always assisted him. I've given you my true confession. Have you ever been in a dominant-submissive relationship? "

"You already know how I lost my virginity to Ruby. After my first divorce, I dated this woman who liked being a submissive. She claimed it was the only way she could climax. At first, I was turned on by it. But I grew tired of it. I didn't want to have to follow a script each time we had sex. I soon got bored with her and broke up."

"Were you ever the submissive?"

"She was always the submissive."

"Did you want to become her submissive, as in your fantasy? I find it interesting a lot of powerful men do like to be dominated in the bedroom."

"Why should it be any different for men? You're a powerful business woman, yet you like it when I dominate you."

"Hmm. I'll race you back to the house; the loser has to be a sex slave for the rest of the day."

Both were panting as Maggie said to John, "I think you slowed down on purpose so I would win."

"You're just a better runner on the sand than I am. Visit me again in San Francisco, and I'll challenge you where it is hilly."

Maggie was dressed in her short denim mini skirt, clingy red sweater, and her cowboy boots. She directed John to wear his button fly jeans, Henley, loafers, and no underwear.

As she tossed him her keys, she said, "You're driving today. Let's stop for lunch at Lulu Buffett's restaurant first. Then we can go to the seafood market and grocery store after lunch. I want you to cook one of your aphrodisiac dinners."

As they walked to the Tahoe, John said, "Thanks for treating me to lunch, Maggie. The shrimp were excellent."

John gathered the produce and spices he needed and grabbed a dozen sunflowers in the floral department. They next stopped at Blalock Seafood to get fresh Gulf red snapper and oysters and then to the ABC liquor store to get some Pernod. John explained it was for an oyster dish he was making. They made it back to The Grotto just after four.

Maggie arranged the sunflowers in a beautiful Aubagne pottery vase. She had bought it in Arles, France, while Sean was on a National Geographic assignment photographing the *Pont Du Gard*.

"After you put the groceries away, you need to shave the stubble off your face. And shower outside. Then go into the loft and put the restraints on the bed; they are in the top drawer next to the bed. Also take out all my toys and have them ready. Put on some music and light the candles. Fill the bathtub with water and lavender bath salts. And when you finish… please get me. I'm going to have some wine on the porch while you get all this ready. John, before you shower, would you be kind enough to take off my boots?"

As he pulled them off, she let her short skirt hike up. "Come over to me." Maggie enjoyed this newfound power John allowed her, something that Sean never allowed her to do. She unbuttoned his fly and sucked on his cock until it was fully engorged like a ripe plum.

"Now, go shower. And by the way, I forgot to tell you the hot water is turned off. Sorry for the inconvenience."

Feeling somewhat guilty for being so bossy to him, Maggie brought him a terrycloth robe and a bath towel. She opened the shower door and said, "How's the shower?"

"It's fine. Would you care to join me?" John picked her up and forced her into the shower.

"Let me down."

"I thought you wanted to come in."

John turned the water off. Maggie's clothes clung to her shivering body; fortunately, she'd taken her boots off. "I'll get you back for this. I'm so infuriated with you."

John couldn't help but laugh as he said, "Let's take off your wet clothes and put on this robe."

Lowering her into her bed, he said, "I know just the way to get you warmed up. Let me put this pillow under your bottom. Part your legs."

He straddled her with his head facing her feet. Teasingly he rubbed his prickly chin over her sensitive inner thighs causing her to giggle. When he rubbed his chin lightly over her clitoris she moaned, "On second thought, perhaps you don't need to shave."

John was busy preparing dinner. He had changed into sweat pants and Berkeley T-Shirt. Barefoot and wearing a sheer lavender gauze caftan, she stood behind him and hugged his muscular waist. *Margaritaville* was playing in the background. John said, "I hope you don't mind; I put on some music. You must have every Jimmy Buffett album ever released."

"What's the world's sexiest chef cooking tonight?"

"A food network inspired dinner. I found the recipes on the internet. To start with, we are having Tyler Florence's *Oysters Rockefeller with a Mignonette Sauce*. You're right, these oysters must be on steroids; they are much bigger than the ones we get on the Pacific Coast. For the entrée, we're having Barefoot Contessa's *Mustard Roasted Red Snapper* and her *Dill Fingerling Potatoes*. Mustard is also an aphrodisiac. Of course you know what snapper is slang for and since Shakespeare's time, potatoes were viewed as an aphrodisiac and labeled the apples of love."

"And dessert?"

"I saw you had a fondue pot, so I made dark chocolate fondue with bananas, figs, and strawberries, the ultimate in aphrodisiac fruits."

"I'm artistically inspired by your dinner menu. Maybe I'll do a painting of this giant plate that appears to be filled with food, but upon closer scrutiny, you will see all types of erotic images."

"It would be an interesting still life."

Maggie could not resist squeezing his cock through his fleece grey sweatpants. "You'd be the perfect model for the giant cucumber. Actually, during the late Renaissance, artists and poets used fruit and vegetables as sexual metaphors; I'm just reversing the idea."

"Keep groping the chef, and your dinner will be delayed. The oysters will be ready in a minute. Since you're my Master, you make the decision."

"This is too contrived; no more role playing."

As he gave her his killer smile, he replied, "But I enjoy watching you try and dominate me."

"For you…this was just a game to see how I would react."

John removed a large broiler pan from the oven. A dozen perfectly cooked oysters bubbled in their shells. "Now these are extremely hot, let me lift several for you from the rock salt. I've some lemon wedges and red pepper sauce."

After Maggie had tasted an oyster, she said, "You sure know how to find the way to my heart. These oysters are wonderful."

The next morning, Maggie couldn't sleep late. She went into the living room to view the pictures John had taken in San Francisco. The expression on her blindfolded face was captivating. The tenseness in her body as he prodded her and clamped her nipples. The ice torture he inflicted upon her.

John pulled on his sweat pants and found Maggie working on her laptop at the dining table. "It's only 5:30 in the morning; why are you up so early?"

"I couldn't sleep. I'm trying to figure out the next painting I should do."

"Let me grab a cup of coffee. Want me to refill your cup?"

"No, thanks."

John took his coffee and sat down at the table.

"Look through these pictures and tell me which is your favorite."

"Without even looking, Nick's Cove in the master bedroom. You're wearing two sets of pearls and the riding crop is next to you. Here it is."

"Why that one?"

"It brings back memories of that special night in New York when you played out my fantasy."

"But unless someone knows what was going on, no one will get it."

"But even so, your pose is extremely erotic. I also liked several of the pictures I took in the Joker's Shed. You looked provocative wearing only pearls and high heels."

"What about the ones you took of me when I was blindfolded?"

"Honestly, I find those the most erotic of all, maybe too much."

"I'm inspired to paint today, would you mind?"

"Not at all, but let's first go for a run on the beach."

133

They were about to turn around from their run when John said, "Let's take a break."

John sat down on the sand, and Maggie sat between his legs. She felt protected as he wrapped his arms across her chest so she could lean back against him.

The beach was deserted except for the squawking sandpipers and seagulls searching for food along the shore.

Maggie broke the silence, "I didn't realize until the other day that seagulls are monogamous."

"Although I've read they have a fairly high divorce rate, twenty-five percent."

Maggie said, "That's depressing. Wonder what causes them to divorce?"

"Incompatibility, a conflict over how long each gets to incubate their eggs. They apparently derive pleasure when they incubate."

"You never talk about what you want out of our relationship."

"You know I have a terrible track record."

"I have too. But that doesn't mean I've given up."

"I think we should take it slowly and not rush into anything. We've known each other for less than two months. I know you're eager to paint, so let's head back. First person to the house gets a massage from the loser."

Maggie said, "I turned the water heater back on. The temperature should be fine." She adjusted the temperature and the pulsing speed of the showerhead and entered the shower. "This feels great. Join me."

"I'll be back in a minute. Don't get too carried away with the massager."

Maggie held the nozzle away from her and turned the water to its coldest setting. When John joined her in the shower, she aimed it at his crotch and said, "Gotcha. I know what you're doing, losing on purpose."

John grabbed her around the waist, gained control of the showerhead and aimed it between her legs. Maggie cried out, "No. No. Stop."

"Maggie O', does this feel good?"

"It's freezing. Stop. The hot water is working. I was just teasing you."

"You were teasing me. How does this feel against your nipples now? Is it teasing them?"

"I'll do anything you want…just stop."

John turned off the water and said, "Alright, I'll tell you what I want tonight. It's time for your massage."

After drying her off, he wrapped Maggie in a large beach towel and spread another towel over the screened porch daybed.

"Lie down on the towel. Are you chilled? I can turn the space heater on."

"That would be great."

"I'll be back shortly. I want to dress and get some massage oil I picked up at the store yesterday."

As John massaged her shoulders and back, he said, "You never told me what happened between you and Sharon at the Stanford Park."

"I'm not bi-sexual, if that's what you're wondering. It was totally innocent."

"But I admit I was turned on when I found Sharon's panties in the hotel bed and imagined the two of you making love."

John moved down to her buttocks. "I've never had my buttocks massaged by a masseuse. It feels good."

Maggie was totally relaxed until he swatted her bottom and said, "Time to roll over."

"Hey, that smarted."

"You deserved more than one swat for what you did in the shower."

"Actually, spanking can be quite a sexual turn on."

"Are you hinting to me?"

Using his bare hand, John spanked her several more times. Maggie screamed. Her bottom was marked, symbolizing her willful submission. "Is this what you've wanted me to do Maggie O'?"

"Yes." She was reduced to a physical creature existing only in the here and now, feeling the pleasurable pain she desperately needed. Each stroke of his hand against her bare skin filled her body and soul with energy. She imagined John being the mortal and she being the mermaid finally able to experience forbidden pleasures. Once he marked her, she was able to experience a greater plateau than ever before.

CHAPTER FOURTEEN

OYSTER PEARL

It was late morning, and Sophie B. Hawkins' *Damn I Wish I Was Your Lover* was playing in the background. Maggie painted a modification of John's first choice, the photo he took in the master bedroom at Nick's Cove. The idea came to her to place her seductive image inside an oyster shell. She had always been fascinated by how pearls are formed as a defense mechanism against an irritant, such as grit or sand. The oyster's natural reaction is to cover up the irritant with layers of the substance that is used to create the shell. At 1 p.m., John knocked on the door. "I brought you a sandwich and some iced tea. I'm getting ready to run to the store. Is there anything you need?"

"Can't think of anything. Thanks for making lunch. Just leave it by the door."

At 7:15 p.m., John knocked once again.

"Maggie enough for today. You need to relax now."

"I'm sorry. I'll be down soon."

She had been painting so intensively that she had no grasp of time. Inspired by her new painting, Maggie changed into both sets of pearls and the bustier she had put in the painting. Wishing to surprise John, she covered up her outfit with her red robe.

As she came down the stairs, Alabama's *Mountain Music* was playing; Maggie had every album Alabama had released. She yelled down, "Something smells incredibly wonderful."

"I'm pan grilling some New Zealand lamb chops. Sit down at the counter. I'll pour you a glass of Merlot."

"I lost track of time."

"Can I see what you've done?"

"Not until I'm finished. What did you do today?"

"Actually, I had a nice day. I finished a book I'd started reading on the plane titled *A World on Fire*. It's about Britain's crucial role in the American Civil War. I want to get another book to read. Is there a bookstore nearby?"

"My favorite one is in Fairhope. I need to go over to the Art Center there to look at a new artist's exhibit whose work I may be interested in launching in New York. Why don't we go there tomorrow?"

"I made special plans for tomorrow night here at the beach."

"We can be back here before then. What have you planned?"

"It's a surprise for you. We need to be back before sunset."

Maggie was washing a dinner plate when John leaned against her. She put the plate on the drying rack and turned around to face him. He appeared to have something hidden behind his back.

"What are you hiding from me?"

He showed her a twelve-inch wooden ruler. A gap in her robe allowed him to see her outfit underneath. As he pinched both her nipples, he said, "You're such a tease."

He whispered in her ear, "Take this ruler with you to the grotto and put your stockings and heels on. I'll be up shortly."

Joining her in the grotto, John said, " It's interesting you sent me the story you wrote about the professor. I read it again today. I believe you're much like the student. Hand me the blindfold."

John blindfolded her and instructed her to brace herself against the dresser. Between each whack with the wooden ruler, he ran his hand up and down the pearls making them brush against her. He watched Maggie's expression reflected in the seashell mosaic mirror she had made. "That was minimum punishment, ten times. Don't forget this pain; I can make it more severe if you continue to displease me."

Maggie welcomed his punishment knowing her true reward would soon follow. John softly kissed her welts, untied her blindfold, and guided her to the bed. He pounded into her. To her, it was sublime, a delicious, addicting combination of lust and pain.

As Maggie arranged her hair into a loose bun, she studied her flush face in the bathroom mirror. She had gone through another metamorphosis, truly exposing her most vulnerable side. What a risky situation she had put herself in. *Why have I opened Pandora's box and exposed my masochism desires?*

She changed out of her outfit, slipped on her red robe, and climbed the stairs. The tub was filled, but he was not upstairs. Three Days Grace's *Pain* playing on her CD player. *That's odd I don't remember buying that CD.* She walked over to the player and found an empty CD cover titled *One-X*. She turned around and was startled as he came through the door with two drinks.

"Let's have some cognac before bed. I picked some up today."

"Did you buy this new CD?"

"I hope you didn't already have it. It came with a free wooden ruler."

"You have a twisted sense of humor. I've listened to it at Matthew's several times."

"I've put some Epsom salts in the bath water for you."

She dropped her robe, stepped into the tub and carefully lowered her chafed skin into the water. As John joined her, he said, "You could almost swim laps in here."

"I know. It was custom made for the honeymoon suite of a new Florida resort development. They went bankrupt, and I got a great deal on the tub. I had it installed in front of this large window so I can see the beach while I soak in it."

"I need to know if I overstepped our boundaries today."

"No. You're the professor I wrote about."

John said, "Is that what you want?"

Maggie blushed. "I think I'll start calling you 'Professor'."

"Just so you aren't confusing me with the art professor."

It was a beautiful morning as they drove through The Grand Hotel's guard gate. Seasonal hanging baskets filled with purple, russet, and yellow pansies dangled from the black iron lampposts marking the long driveway to the hotel. The majestic canopy of Southern Live Oaks, Southern Magnolias, and Longleaf Pines shaded the perfectly manicured grounds. The Southern Indian azalea bushes were beginning to show their stunning blooms.

"Our area is famous for our azaleas. My favorite are the beautiful magenta colored ones, called, 'Formosa'. When they are in full bloom, you can see them a mile away. Isn't it beautiful here?"

"Extremely. These live oak trees are incredible. I like how the Spanish moss hangs down from them."

As they walked into the lobby, Maggie said, "This hotel has quite a history. It was destroyed in a fire. It was used as a Civil War hospital and then as a training base for the Army Air Corps during World War II. It's been through numerous hurricanes including Frederic and Katrina. It flooded during Katrina. Fortunately, they reopened it after a $50 million renovation."

They sat at a table next to the windows with a view of the hotel's boardwalk and fishing pier. Identical twin boys were playing croquet on the outside lawn as their parents cheered them on.

Maggie said, "Those boys are so cute. It must be neat to have twins."

"Thanks for suggesting we stop here for breakfast. This place makes me think I've stepped back in time. When I've time to read, I enjoy reading about historical battles. Last summer while I vacationed with my kids, I read about Rear Admiral David G. Farragut and the Battle of Mobile Bay. Mobile Bay was the last important port east of the Mississippi River remaining in Confederate possession. Its closure was important to the Union."

"If you come back, we should go to Fort Morgan and then take the ferry over to see Fort Gaines on Dauphin Island. But right now, unless you want to battle with me, let's get something to eat. I'm famished. I prefer to order off the menu, although the breakfast buffet is good too."

"I'll have whatever you're having."

"I always order the Oscar Benedict, which has lump crab meat, and have the local stone ground grits. The potatoes are good if the grits are too Southern for you."

"I'm a risk taker."

They finished breakfast, and Maggie showed John the hotel's special art collection. "Nall is an internationally recognized artist. He attended *École des Beaux-Arts* in Paris and was mentored by Salvador Dali. This painting was done after Hurricane Katrina. I love how he incorporated washed up hurricane debris."

"He is extremely talented."

"The Art Center should be open now. Why don't we head over? I got an email from this regional artist who is interested in working with us. He's a friend of another artist I've helped launch."

Maggie was impressed with the artist's refreshing panache. He had a unique approach, a mixed media pointillism style. As they finished looking at his exhibit Maggie turned to John, "So what do you think about his work?"

John said, "I like this one especially where he used old car tags and street signs in his composition."

"I can think of several art collectors who would buy this. Let's go to Page and Palette; you can get a book to read. It amazes me the number of writers who live in Fairhope, per capita they probably have the largest concentration of writers in the country."

With Maggie's encouragement, John found two great books, *Forest Gump* and *Vicksburg 1863,* both written by Winston Groom, a famous local writer.

"Why don't you take a break from reading historical stuff and read *Forest Gump*. Have you seen the movie with Tom Hanks?"

"The only time I go to see a movie is with my kids."

"After you read the book, we should rent the movie. Let's walk around town. There are some great shops and galleries here."

"Let's put the books in the car."

As they walked to Maggie's Tahoe, John noticed a wine shop across the street. "Do you mind if we go into that wine shop?"

Thirty minutes later John put a case of wine in the back of the Tahoe. Maggie asked him, "Why did you buy so much wine? It's already Tuesday, and you're leaving Friday."

"Hopefully, you'll invite me to come back. Don't serve any of these to your girlfriends. Give them that Skinny Bitch wine. These bottles are for our special times together."

"I know we had a big breakfast, but I'm getting hungry, and you know how ornery I get when I'm hungry. Let's get something to eat. There's a wonderful new Lebanese place a few blocks down. I love their garlic labneh."

"Sure let's walk there. Fairhope reminds me of several of the quaint towns in The Napa Valley."

"I almost moved here instead of rebuilding at the beach."

"Why did you change your mind?"

"I enjoy the solitude I feel at the beach."

"Would you mind if we first walk over to that cigar store we passed coming into town?"

"Sure. I didn't know you smoked cigars?"

"You still have a lot to learn about me."

On their way back to her house, Maggie was surprised when John drove into the parking lot of the tallest beachside condo building on West Beach Boulevard. Puzzled she asked him, "Why are we parking here?"

"Watching the sunset."

"We can watch it at my place."

"It doesn't meet the requirements of what I've planned."

He opened the car door for Maggie and said, "You have your choice; take the elevator up to the twenty-sixth floor, or we can walk up the stairwell?"

When Maggie entered the elevator, John said, "Push twenty-six, the penthouse floor."

This time John chose not to distract Maggie as they rode up the elevator. He witnessed her unmasked fear, as sweat formed on her brow and her breathing shortened.

There were only two condos on the penthouse level. John had reserved the one with a western view.

Maggie calmed down once she walked inside. She noticed her picnic basket was sitting on the kitchen counter. "Is this where you went this morning?"

John took a bottle of champagne out of the refrigerator. "Let's have some champagne and sit on the balcony."

"Why did you want to bring me here? You know I hate heights."

"I also know how the tension increases your excitement. Get undressed and join me on the side balcony; the sun will be setting soon."

"But it's chilly outside."

Maggie removed her clothes and wrapped a bath towel around her. She found John reclining in a lounge chair smoking a cigar. On the table beside him was the twelve-inch wooden ruler.

As the sun disappeared in the horizon, John picked up the ruler and tapped it against his palm. "Now take the towel off. Go over to the railings and face the water."

Maggie had an adrenalin rush as she moved towards the rail. As she had done before on John's deck, she braced herself against the rail. She could feel her heart pounding as John lubricated her bum.

"Take one of your hands off the rail and touch yourself."

"I can't." Once again, she flinched as the ruler marked her flesh. "I'm scared."

"Maggie O', you know better than to disobey me. Now let go."

Maggie shook all over as her right hand let go of the rail and stroked herself. The ripping sound of John unzipping his jeans made her breathing quicken. Holding her steady, John said, "Now let go of the rail with your other hand and try and relax."

As her Professor fully impaled her, nothing else mattered; Maggie's fear transformed into carnal lust.

CHAPTER FIFTEEN

TATOOS

Just before five, Maggie was singing along with Sade's *Paradise* while signing her new painting. When she turned off the CD player, she heard John downstairs. She changed into her favorite Alabama sweatshirt and yoga pants and called down to him, "I've finally finished. Do you want to see it?"

John hurried up the stairs. As she aimed a spotlight on her latest painting, John studied it for a minute.

Maggie nervously awaited his comment, "Well, what do think?"

"It's so sensual; I'm buying it."

"I appreciate your interest, but I need this piece for my exhibit, if I do one."

"I'll be the highest bidder, I assure you."

His approval always pleased her. "You're not just saying that?"

"Come here." He pulled her tightly against him.

She unzipped his jeans and said, "Let me take care of that." She pouted at him like a child, "Please?"

"Part of this punishment is denying you that pleasure. I'm teaching you a lesson. Besides, you took care of me last night and this morning."

"I prefer you as The Professor and not Caligula."

"Why not Caligula, the Roman Emperor? He was notorious for his sexual bacchanalias and insatiable lust. Let's have a glass of wine while I cook the steaks."

"I like this wine."

"It's a Cab I picked up at that wine store. I opened it earlier so it would have a chance to breathe. How do you want your steak cooked?"

"Medium rare."

"I got us a movie to watch tonight. *Forest Gump*. I would have gotten *Caligula* had I known you were a fan."

After dinner, Maggie put the movie in the DVD player and cuddled next to John on the sofa. Having had a little too much wine, she dozed off right after Forest proposed to Jenny.

"Maggie, wake up. The movie is over. Let's go to bed."

She opened her eyes, and he was standing naked next to her with a fully erect cock. She sat up and was ready to suck him dry. He pulled her away and looked deeply into her eyes, "It's time to finish our earlier business. Let's go into the grotto."

Maggie stripped as she walked ahead of John. She turned her iPod on, and Sophie B. Hawkins' sultry voice filled the room as she sang, *Damn I Wish I Was Your Lover*. Maggie seductively reclined back on the bed with her knees up and parted, sensually touching her erect nipples. "Please finish me now."

John positioned himself between her open knees and tortured her with his teeth and tongue. He enjoyed bringing her to near climax and abruptly stopping. He continued this pattern until Maggie had no more tolerance left. She begged him to make her come. Finally, he put her out of her misery, causing her to reach an earth trembling climax. Blanketed in sweat, they quietly rested for several minutes.

The next morning Maggie put on her robe and found John preoccupied on his laptop. Not wanting to disturb him, she poured herself a cup of coffee and walked outside to the screened porch. It was chilly; she turned on the outdoor heater. John going back to California saddened her mood.

John opened the door leading to the porch. "Can I join you?"

"It's a little chilly, but I love to hear the waves. It clears the cobwebs from my mind. This past week has gone by way too fast."

"*Carpe diem.*"

"Seize the day?"

"Yes. Let's make the most of today. I looked up the weather, and it's supposed to get up to seventy-two degrees. I propose we could go to that deserted part of the beach and study the seagulls again. Only this time, we'll bring a blanket and a picnic."

John removed his t-shirt and said, "I should try and get some sun today; people will wonder if I really vacationed at the beach."

"You need to be careful and not get sunburned. I've sunscreen; would you like some?"

"Not yet."

"Suit yourself." Maggie pulled off her t-shirt and revealed her lavender halter-top. She opened the top to the sunscreen.

John said, "You don't need this." He untied the neck and unhooked the back. "Now hand me the lotion and lie down."

Maggie lay back on the blanket, and John methodically spread lotion on her arms and shoulders. "Take your shorts off too."

"I don't have anything under them."

"Good. Less to take off."

John pulled them down and spread more lotion on her legs moving seductively upward to her thighs, her pelvis area and upward to her abdomen.

He purposely saved her chest for last. As he attended to her chest, he rolled her nipples. "You need to be protected here. You don't want these to get burned. Your front is done. Let's have some champagne before I get your backside." As they toasted, he said, "Carpe diem."

After they both devoured bagels with cream cheese and smoked salmon John said, "Have you ever wanted to get a tattoo?"

"When I was younger. How about you?"

"I've been in such a conservative profession. But my attitude has changed. I can see a butterfly placed right above your tailbone."

"And if I agreed to do so, would you get one?"

"I would."

"What type of tattoo would you get?"

"Let me draw it for you."

John used a piece of driftwood to draw in the sand, Δ 211.

Maggie wrapped a beach towel around her and walked over to him. "What does that mean?"

"It was our cancelled Delta flight. Let's do it before I head back."

"You're not serious?"

"Quite serious." John pulled off his running shorts, and Maggie imagined he wanted to have sex as he jerked her beach towel off of her. But instead he scooped her up in his arms and walked towards the water. "I've been dying to do this."

"What are you doing? Put me down."

A large wave headed directly towards them as he walked deeper into the chilled water. He kneeled as the wave crashed against them, knocking him down and pushing them back towards the beach.

Maggie shouted, "Are you crazy?"

148

"Indeed I am." He kissed her and held her tightly. John lifted her up and carried her back to the blanket.

Maggie lost the coin toss. She would go first. She had decided she wanted a Painted Lady butterfly. Jim, the tattooed-cover artist, was also a contemporary mixed media artist who had received his Bachelor of Fine Arts degree from Auburn University. After he had finished tattooing Maggie, he showed her photos of several of his paintings.

"You're talented. Let me help you market your work; I have a gallery in New York."

"You aren't that famous artist, Maggie O', that paints erotic self-portraits?"

"Guilty."

"I'm honored to have inked your body. Anytime you want additional tattoos, please let me know; I will do them for free. I also do body piercings, if you're interested."

"Do you mind if I watch you tattoo my friend?"

"No, not at all."

CHAPTER SIXTEEN

FAIRY TALE BELIEFS

It was Saturday, the first day after John had returned home. While lounging in bed, Maggie anxiously checked her phone to see if he had contacted her.

"Missing your butterfly tattoo."

She opened the attachment and found a picture of her naked tush and her tattoo. She took a picture with her cell phone of her empty bed in the grotto and sent it to him.

"Missing you in bed."

"Call me now."

"It was the loneliest east to west coast flight I've ever experienced. Come stay with me and work on your next painting here."

"You know I have to go to New York to help out at the gallery while Matthew's mother is having rotator cuff surgery. He'll be in Chicago taking care of her."

The phone line went silent for almost a minute.

Maggie defensively said, "I don't have any other choice in the manner. Matthew tried unsuccessfully to get his mom to come to New York for the surgery."

"I've been postponing a business trip to Asia. I'll go ahead and schedule it. Perhaps we can get together next month."

Guilt overcame her, when they hung up. *See what happens when you start getting too close in a relationship.*

While searching for the partnership income tax records, Maggie came across a folder labeled, *The Nymph's Exhibit*. Inside the folder, she found a sales invoice with a copy of a check signed by Christopher T. Marshall. She didn't remember seeing Chris at the exhibit. Matthew had mentioned this attractive Aussie had bought her two paintings. It never crossed her mind that it was Chris. *But why would he have bought these two erotic paintings if he were married? It was hard to imagine someone's wife allowing that. Had he gotten a divorce?*

Maggie woke up next to John in his New York condo. He had surprised her the day before by flying in from Hong Kong. Restless, she went into the living room to check her messages. She saw several missed calls from Matthew and a text message as well.

"Call me. It's urgent!"

Immediately she called Matthew.

"Sharon was in a terrible automobile accident last night. She was hit by a DUI driver on her way home from work."

I must be having a horrible dream. "Matthew, tell me she's okay."

"I'm sorry, but she didn't survive."

John woke up to Maggie screaming. He rushed over to her and grabbed her in his arms. "What's wrong?"

She was speechless as she handed him her phone.

John said, "Who is this?"

"This is Matthew. Sharon was killed in an automobile accident last night. Her car was hit by a DUI."

"Sharon is like a sister to Maggie. What do we need to do?"

"Sharon doesn't have any close blood relatives."

"I need to get back to Maggie. I'll call you later."

"Maggie, it's time to get up. I've found out that you're the executor of Sharon's estate, and you need to meet her attorney, Maria Stone, in Rutherford. You have an appointment with her Monday. You'll need to fly out with me today. Even though I have to be in Palm Springs for that conference next week, you can stay at my place and use my car."

For convenience, Maggie stayed at Sharon's place. John called her Monday night after her meeting.

"How did your meeting go?"

"Fortunately, Sharon left detailed instructions in her will. She'd already arranged to have her body donated to medical research. The proceeds of her estate go to her foundation. She also requested that I oversee the foundation."

"How long do you think you'll be in Napa?"

"It's hard to say. I need to list her townhouse, sell her car, and her other personal property. I also have to deal with her foundation. I called Matthew and told him to delay my exhibit indefinitely."

"Are you sure you're not postponing it for other reasons?"

"I couldn't paint right now if someone held a gun to my head. I forgot to tell you that the New Hope Clinic has commissioned me to paint a portrait of Sharon. Just last week Sharon sent me the photograph she'd selected for me to use."

Maggie wished she could cry. "Everything is so screwed up now. Sharon's sudden death has made me question what I'm doing with my own life right now. John, I need a break for a while. After I finish here, I'm going back to Gulf Shores."

Back in Gulf Shores, Maggie met with Dr. Harris, her psychiatrist. She had been seeing him off and on since college.

"How have you been Maggie? It's been over a year since your last session."

"I feel like cutting myself again. I made a promise to Sharon that I would never do it again. And now she's gone. It's so unfair that after being cancer free for six years, this drunk jerk slammed into her car."

Maggie went on to tell Dr. Harris about her latest relationship. "I'm always attracted to the wrong guys. John's been divorced three times. He's not looking for a commitment. I'm just an easy lay for him.

"And now Chris has written a book based on the summers he spent with me at the beach. He sent me a copy of it. He wants to explain what happened."

"You told me last year that you've never stopped loving Chris. How do you feel now since he is reaching out to you again?"

"It would be wrong for me to see him again."

"Why? Seeing him would possibly bring closure, whatever ultimately happens."

"But what about my relationship with John?"

"I think you might be too presumptuous about him. I've known people who marry the fourth time and are quite happy. From what you told me, he makes a lot of effort to be with you. If he wanted only a sex object, I'm sure there are plenty of women in San Francisco who would oblige him."

"John is an amazing person, but I'm scared."

"Why are you scared?"

"That I'm incapable of being loved. I feel like the only person who loved me unconditionally was Sharon and now I've lost her."

"Maggie, don't blame yourself; you grew up in a dysfunctional family with no one there to show you what a committed, loving relationship was. Your mother was such a narcissist; she had nothing left for you. Your maid, Bessie, was more of a mother to you. Your dad remarried when you were only six and moved over a thousand miles away from you."

Back at her cottage, she aimlessly watched the kitchen counter television while she ate a pimento cheese sandwich for lunch. A local TV host, Dixie Reynolds, was talking about her next guest. Once a news anchor for a Birmingham television station, Dixie had married a wealthy Gulf Shores developer and moved to Ono Island at the age of thirty-two.

Dixie said, "I'm privileged to have Christopher T. Marshall with us today. Chris is the author of *My Innocent Mermaid*, a new controversial book set in our own Gulf Shores area."

Maggie's heart raced as she stared intently at the small TV screen. *Damn, Chris is still a sexy hunk.*

Dixie said, "Chris, I read your story and I honestly felt unsettled, but moved by the coming of age relationship you wrote about."

Chris replied in his true Aussie accent, "I'm glad you felt that way. Life isn't always an easy and defined path. I feel relationships are the same way. My characters were pure in the love they found for each other. It was the outside pressures that were toxic."

Dixie said, "Many people are trying to speculate in real life who your dysfunctional characters are based on, especially this innocent mermaid you wrote about."

Chris smiled and bowed his head slightly before he answered her. "I guess I've done a great job as a fiction writer for people to be concerned if I'm writing about them. But I certainly haven't seen any mermaids in a long time around here have you?"

"But do you think mermaids still exist?"

Chris had baited Dixie as he reeled her in further. "I think of a mermaid as a special metaphor for an enchanting woman, someone much like you Dixie."

Dixie tried to compose herself as she continued her scripted interview. "We have spoken to several local people who said you spent summers in the late Wanda Beauregard O'Reilly's cottage."

"Wanda's father and my grandfather were once business associates, and Wanda and I were like cousins to one another."

Irritated Maggie stated, "More like cousins with conjugal rights. Please don't get my family involved in this."

Flustered and ready to end the interview Dixie said, "I see you have a book signing this afternoon at Page and Palette in Fairhope."

"Yes. I'll be there from three to five."

She struggled with what she should wear; she didn't want to look too eager. She settled on wearing her distressed Calvin Klein skinny jeans and her favorite lavender J.Crew cardigan. It would have been a conservative look for her if she had not left so many buttons undone. She couldn't believe it had been thirteen years since she last saw him; much had happened since.

When Maggie arrived at 4:30 p.m., the line outside Page and Palette snaked past Mr. Gene's Beans on De La Mare Avenue. As others arrived to get their books autographed, she purposely kept stepping back to the end of the line. She wore her Ray-Ban sunglasses and had her hair tucked underneath her white straw Panama Jack hat. She hoped no one would recognize her. She still could not believe Chris had become an overnight sensation because of his controversial book based on a young Southern teenager coming of age with an older man from Australia. The things that made Chris's book most interesting were the subplots that involved the people who threw stones while they lived their own contradictory lives.

When she finally made her way to the front of the line, he looked up and froze as he gazed at her.

"Maggie."

"So my disguise didn't work?"

"There is no way you could disguise yourself from me. Can we go somewhere after my signing and catch up, have dinner perhaps?"

"Come by my place; we'll have some wine first. You can follow me, since you probably won't recognize the place. I had it rebuilt after Hurricane Ivan destroyed it."

"You go ahead while I finish here. I remember where you live. I drove by it yesterday; it's painted lavender, your favorite color, and there's a sign out front that says, *Mermaid's Grotto.*"

Maggie looked down to see if he was wearing a wedding band. He didn't have one on, but that didn't mean he wasn't still married.

She was a nervous wreck, when he finally arrived. He had brought a bottle of Moet & Chandon *White Star Champagne* and a bouquet of cut lavender tied with a lavender gingham ribbon.

"Smells so good; I love lavender. Let me put these in a vase and open the champagne."

Chris said, "Do you mind if I put some music on?"

"Go ahead. My CD's are in the top drawer."

Chris put on Elton John's *Something About The Way You Look Tonight.*

Maggie said, "That's one of my favorite songs."

"Every time I hear it, I think of you."

After thirty minutes of small talk, Maggie got the courage to ask Chris, "Why have you shown up in my life after so many years? I'd heard you got married."

156

"That was a long time ago; I was trapped by a college student. She told me she was pregnant. She said she would accuse me of raping her if I didn't marry her, ending my academic career. Two months later, she miscarried."

"How horrible."

"I found out the baby couldn't have been mine. The autopsy report indicated the fetus was five months old. With my knowing that she'd lied about my being the father, she agreed to a divorce and moved back in with her previous boyfriend."

"So when you came to my art exhibit, you were divorced. You bought two of my paintings. Why didn't you come over to me at the exhibit?"

"I had intended to, but I overheard someone say that your lover had taken the photos you used for your paintings. I didn't want to screw up your relationship with him."

"Ironically, I ended that relationship that same night."

"That summer your mother caught us, we should have run away together. Maggie, I've never stopped loving you."

He unbuttoned her cardigan and pressed his full lips against her supple nipple. Maggie had a flashback of that innocent day during the summer of 1998 when Chris had first kissed her.

As she pulled away, she said, "I'm sorry, Chris. This isn't right. I realize I've been holding on to fairy tale beliefs far too long, hoping the ending in your book would actually happen. I'm not that innocent mermaid anymore."

"Do you love someone else?"

"Honestly, I'm not sure."

The next morning Maggie took a brisk walk. Low tide exposed a wide swath of the beach. The sandpipers and seagulls squawked at each other as they scavenged for their breakfast. Reaching into her jean pocket, she removed her grandfather's pocketknife. As she pressed the knife's blade into the flesh of

157

her left wrist, the memory of losing her dearest friend overwhelmed her. She slowly lifted the blade away and dropped the knife into the sand. In a trance-like state, Maggie fell to her knees, as she thought she heard the voice of Sharon calling to her in the distance. Remembering the promise she made to Sharon, she picked up the pocketknife, pressed the handle button, and closed the blade.

The following day, Maggie called Mary and asked her to come over to help pack some items she wanted to give away. Mary was shocked when she saw boxes and garbage bags piled in the middle of the floor.

"Holy moly, girl, what are you doing?"

"I'm purging my life, getting rid of anything that has an unpleasant memory attached to it."

"You're giving away your silver, crystal, and china? And this beautiful vase you bought in France?"

"Take anything you want; otherwise, I'm taking it to the thrift store."

"My niece, Kim, just graduated from college. She would love these clothes; she's about your size. My nephew, John, is in Boy Scouts. He would probably like this pocket knife."

"Please take them."

"What about your jewelry, especially your pearls?"

"Those pearls belonged to my mother."

"Are you sure you're not acting irrationally?"

"I've never been more rational in my life."

"Speaking of moods, how is your relationship going with John?"

"We've taken a sabbatical."

CHAPTER SEVENTEEN

A NEW WORLD IS BORN

John was excited when he received an invitation to the reception unveiling Maggie's painting. After Sharon's death, he donated $10,000 to New Hope Clinic in her memory. The five months since he and Maggie had been apart had distressed him. He constantly pondered why Sharon's death had caused Maggie to push him away. When they were at The Grand Hotel, he sensed she had a strong maternal instinct. He had been afraid to tell her he had gotten a vasectomy after the twins were born. Recently he consulted with a urologist about having his vasectomy reversed.

It was Friday, September 19, 2014. Maggie had chosen to wear her infamous red dress to the New Hope Clinic reception. Painting her deceased friend had been both an emotional and artistic challenge. She'd almost reneged on doing the commission. Then she remembered how excited Sharon was about the project. Sharon wanted to be portrayed as Elpis, The Greek Goddess of Hope. Elpis, along with all the other daimones, was trapped in a jar by Zeus and entrusted to the care of Pandora. When Pandora opened the vessel, all of the guardian spirits escaped except for Elpis; she remained to comfort mankind.

For her life-size portrait, Sharon wore an ankle-length Doric chiton. The fuchsia wool sleeveless tunic was clasped at her left shoulder exposing her right breast and scar. She wore it cinched

159

at the waist with a large belt called a 'zoster'. Sharon had added ringlet hair extensions and wore a hair wreath made from pink sweetheart roses, grape leaves, and berries. She held a European-style bouquet of six Rose of Sharon blooms which symbolized the six years since her surgery.

Dr. Roberts had asked Maggie to give a brief speech before the unveiling of Sharon's portrait. Standing next to the painting, he said, "It's my pleasure to introduce you to Maggie O'Reilly, the artist commissioned to paint this special portrait of Sharon Richards. About a year ago, I read an article that Maggie wrote on how art had healed Sharon. Last December, I was attending a meeting in New York and went by Maggie's gallery to see Sharon's work. Moved by her art, I bought all sixty paintings; which hang on the wall behind me."

The guests started applauding. After a minute, he continued, "Please welcome, Maggie O'Reilly."

"Thank you Dr. Roberts for opening up your heart and your pocketbook in support of my dearest friend, Sharon Richards, a brave breast cancer survivor. Unfortunately she was the victim of a DUI driver. Otherwise, she would be with us tonight unveiling this portrait she envisioned.

"When I think of Sharon, I think of one of my favorite authors, Anaïs Nin, who shared a similar Bohemian lifestyle to Sharon's. *In The Diary of Anaïs Nin (Vol. 1: 1931-1934)* she wrote, *Each friend represents a world in us, a world possibly not born until they arrive, and it is only by this meeting that a new world is born.*

"This was the type of friend Sharon was to me. I became reborn because of her. It was such a privilege to be Sharon's friend and for her to ask me to paint her portrait. Dr. Roberts, if you could assist me with the unveiling."

After the unveiling, other cancer survivors asked Maggie if they could commission her to paint their portraits. Maggie reasoned that these commissions would be another revenue source for Sharon's foundation. Her mood was lifted as she went over to the bar. She grabbed a glass of champagne, stepped back, and accidentally bumped into someone. Before she had a chance to turn around and apologize, she heard a modulated voice say, "Well that's a nice way to be greeted."

That too familiar ache in her heart and desire in her loins returned. She turned around; there he was, wearing his bright red Burberry tie. "John, what are you doing here?"

"I was invited. You've ignored my calls and texts."

"I've been real busy managing Sharon's Foundation, painting this commission, along with my work at the gallery. I figured you were busy with your kids this summer."

John recognized one of the clinic partners walking over to her, the same guy he'd caught Maggie with at the last reception.

Dr. Andrews placed his right hand in the small of Maggie's back, "Fabulous job, Maggie."

"Jim, this is John Kramer. He's a friend of mine from San Francisco."

Jim reluctantly removed his hand from her back and held it out towards John and arrogantly said, "I'm Dr. Andrews. So nice of you to come all the way from San Francisco to be at our reception."

John's much larger hand firmly shook the doctor's hand. With quick wit, John replied, "I would have traveled around the world if I had to. I collect Maggie's art. In fact, I'm in the process of buying several of her newer paintings."

Maggie said, "John, you're being presumptuous that my other paintings are for sale."

"That's one of the reasons I wanted to see you tonight. I have a proposal for you. I'll make a matching donation to Sharon's foundation for whatever amount you sell me your paintings."

Maggie smiled back. "Your offer is tempting."

John said, "Can we discuss this over dinner tonight?"

"I already have plans tonight. A group of us are going out to dinner at Baumé. Would you like to join us?"

Jim interrupted her, "Maggie, it's a small restaurant. I'm not sure we'll have room at our table for John."

John placed his hand on Maggie's shoulder, "That's alright. We can discuss this later over the phone."

Maggie said, "Could I meet you afterwards, for a night cap?"

"I'm staying at the Stanford Park Hotel. Text me when you're leaving the restaurant."

Maggie made an excuse to leave dinner before the dessert course. It was already eleven when she found John waiting for her at the bar. She walked over to him and said, "Excuse me, is this seat taken?"

"It is now; please have a seat. Would you care for a drink?'

"What are you having?"

 "A Bushwacker."

Maggie laughed. "Funny, you remind me of someone I once knew, but they would never drink something so unhealthy and fattening."

"He sounds boring."

"He made up for it in the bedroom."

"What happened?"

"I had a lot of unresolved personal issues that I needed to take care of, and he'd been burned in three marriages already."

"Perhaps your friend is afraid to make a commitment."

"Why?"

"Because he sensed you wanting to have children and he couldn't."

Maggie couldn't believe what he had just said. "Yes, I want a family one day, but I would not mind adopting. Parenting is much more than the DNA you share with your children."

John was elated by her response. "I might drive over to Nick's Cove tomorrow and spend the night there. Would you care to join me?"

"I just met you. You're a stranger."

"What's wrong with being strangers again?"

"Why don't I come to your room tonight and give you my answer in the morning?"

CHAPTER EIGHTEEN

AULD LANG SYNE

It was New Year's Eve, which coincided with Maggie's thirty-second birthday. John was in Vail, Colorado, skiing with his kids while she was in New York getting ready for a new gallery exhibit. Maggie found Matthew at their favorite Café Boulud table.

He gasped, "Oh, my God, you're wearing your Agent Provocateur *Thora* dress."

Midway through their dinner, Maggie said, "Not a day goes by that I don't think of Sharon. Last New Year's Eve, while in Puerto Vallarta, we made a pact to live in the moment, and now she isn't here anymore."

Matthew squeezed Maggie's hand and said, "Sharon would be so proud of the commissions you're doing."

Maggie resisted the urge to cry. "Even before the accident, she was a victim. She'd finally had the courage to start dating again. She attracted this weasel of a man. Let me take that back; he doesn't deserve being called a man. He made her feel like she was a freak for not having reconstructive surgery."

Matthew said, "What a prick."

"Speaking of pricks, tell me about your breakup with Joseph."

"He found a rich sugar daddy. The guy he's seeing is married and CEO of a Fortune 100 corporation. I obviously can't compete with that."

"Money is a powerful aphrodisiac."

"Why can't I find the right partner? I'll be thirty-four soon and, before you know it, I'll have lost my edge. Oh, I forgot to tell you, I read *the book*."

"What book?"

"*My Innocent Mermaid.*"

"Oh, that book."

"How accurate was the story?"

"What he wrote was the PG-13 version."

"Alright, let's go to your room, order an expensive bottle of Champagne, get smashed, and you can tell me the true, uncut version."

Maggie felt ready to return to warmer weather. When you are raised in the Sunbelt, it is hard to acclimate to colder weather, the main reason she had not moved to New York. When she woke up at her beach cottage, it was one of the few winter mornings the temperature was below forty degrees. She waited for it to warm up to the fifties before she jogged along the deserted snow-like white sand beach. Too cold for the normal beachcombers hunting for shells, her only company were the seagulls and sandpipers searching for their next meal. Memories of John, jogging along with her, made her long to be with him again.

After her jog, she drank a protein shake and ran a few errands. When she returned home in the early afternoon, there was a long rectangular box from The Bouqs Company outside her door. She took the box inside and opened it finding fifteen sunflowers and five bunches of green solidago. Maggie smiled when she read the card out loud, "Happy Δ 211". Glancing at her cell phone calendar, she realized it was January 5. She texted him. *"Thank you for the flowers. I hope you're having a great time skiing. I miss you!"*

Maggie's phone rang.

"You don't know how much I miss you. I wish you could have come with us."

"There is no way I'll ever get on a ski lift."

"You could go snowshoeing or just hang at the lodge."

"Maybe next time."

"I can't believe how things have gotten complicated, that we can't be together before I leave again for Hong Kong next week. I'm glad we are hiring a manager for the new branch; I won't have to spend as much time there."

"You're definitely spending a lot of time on it."

"My last trip I would have stayed and finished the project, except it was my turn to have Jack and Annie for New Year's week. Can you believe they turned thirteen last month? It's time for you to meet them; they both want to meet you."

"I'm looking forward to meeting them during their summer break. My half-brother, Colin, will be turning seven soon. I enjoyed being with him over Christmas. How long will you be gone this time?"

"I'm not sure. I've engaged a realtor to look for office space and I have to hire a managing partner. Why don't you come see me?"

"You know I barely survive the flights when I come to San Francisco. Although I have traveled to Europe with the help of an array of drugs and alcohol."

"Take several of your toys to distract you."

"I've got my hands full right now. You won't believe the number of portrait commissions I'm getting. Perhaps it's best that you're going away for a while so I can get caught up."

"Honestly, I think you're burning the candle at both ends, between your commissions and the gallery."

"*You're* telling *me* to avoid burning the candle at both ends? When you do, let me know your secret."

"Look, I've missed you."

"I've missed you too. When you get back, stay with me at the beach. Let's get another tattoo."

"I have an idea. Are you free this weekend?"

"What do you have in mind?"

"Reacquainting ourselves at the Atlanta Ritz Carlton. I'll change my flight reservations to leave for Hong Kong from Atlanta. I have a meeting in my office on Friday. I'll leave that evening and wake you up the next morning. We can spend Saturday and Sunday together. I'm getting a hard-on just thinking about seeing you again."

"Hong Kong is closer to San Francisco than to Atlanta."

"I could care less. Something has to change. Telephone sex and cold showers aren't working."

Samuel waited curbside at the airport for his favorite female customer. He liked how she always had a beautiful smile on her face and how she greeted him with a hug and a peck on his cheek. He was happy for his favorite male customer to be romantically involved with her; they were a perfect match. If he were Mr. Kramer, he would have already popped the question to her. *What's he waiting around for?*

"Good morning, Miss Maggie. I hope you had a pleasant flight."

Maggie hugged him and kissed his cheek. "It was fine, thanks to Xanax. How have you been Samuel? John told me you're now pastor of your church. Congratulations. Are those church ladies still chasing after you?"

"You know I'm saving myself for you Miss Maggie; just don't let Mr. Kramer know that. Now let me help you with your bags."

"Thank you, Samuel."

"You're most welcome. You look so lovely today in that green dress. It matches your sparkling emerald eyes."

167

"You certainly know how to flatter a girl. Would you mind dropping me off at Houston's on Lenox Road and then take my bags to the downtown Ritz and check them with the bellman?"

Samuel opened the back right door for her. She slid inside, surprised when she saw him, wearing his bright red Burberry tie. That sensual ache in her heart and the desire in her loins returned. How she'd missed his brooding brown eyes and the slight scar that trailed up his cheek. She recalled how she asked him about his scar one day, and he simply replied *playing hockey.* She often wondered if that was the truth, since she had covered up the truth about her own scars.

John said, "I would be happy to check your bags for you."

"You came in a day early."

"I rescheduled my meeting to yesterday and took a red-eye flight out. I didn't want to wait another day to see you."

"I wish I would have known you were coming early; I wouldn't have scheduled a lunch appointment. Why don't you join Ryan and me for lunch?"

"I wouldn't want to interfere. Besides, I need a nap. I hardly slept on the plane and I probably won't sleep that much tonight. Here is your keycard."

Maggie raised her right eyebrow and said, "You booked us on the twentieth floor knowing how afraid I'm of heights?"

John shrugged his shoulders, "It's my favorite suite."

"I'll text you when I'm headed back; you'll need to meet me in the lobby."

Annoyed with him for not meeting her in the lobby, she texted him.

"Am I going to have to discipline you tonight for disobeying my request?"

"Is that a promise?"

"I'll be in the lobby bar until you come down."

"I'm waiting for you with a chilled bottle of Dom Perignon and a stiff cock. Where would you rather be? Walk up the stairs if you don't want to ride the elevator."

While waiting on the lobby elevator, Maggie stood behind a couple with a redheaded young boy. When the doors opened, Maggie took a deep breath and followed them inside.

The boy stood guard by the elevator buttons; he grinned at Maggie revealing his missing front tooth and said, "I got a visit from the tooth fairy last night. She gave me ten quarters."

Maggie said, "Wow. You racked up, I only got one quarter when I lost my front tooth."

The father said, "Inflation."

Maggie waited to see what floor they were headed to, hoping it would be at least to her level. The boy's father told the boy to push sixteen.

The father turned to Maggie and said, "And you, Ma'am?"

"Same as yours."

The young boy bounced around and counted aloud each floor they passed, fueling Maggie's anxiety. She practically held her breath the entire time and was relieved when the shiny brass doors opened. She found the sixteenth floor stairwell, took the stairs up to the twenty-fourth floor, used her keycard to enter the room, and found John seated in one of the club chairs in front of a bay window.

Without saying a word, Maggie walked over to John and turned around. He stood up and pressed against her back. His hard-on made it obvious to her what he wanted. He lowered the long decorative gold zipper, exposing her bare back and nude thong.

She allowed her dress to drop to the floor then teasingly turned around. Shielding her nipples with her hands, she sauntered into the marble bathroom shutting the door behind her.

Having gotten her point across, Maggie filled the oversized soaking tub with hot water adding Asprey Purple Water Shower Gel. A citrus ginger aroma infused the steamy room. Maggie turned on her Pandora station and Adele's *Someone Like You* started playing as she slid underneath the water. Listening to the lyrics reminded her of her two former lovers, Christopher and Sean.

She was starting to relax when John entered the opened the door with two flutes of champagne.

"Don't think you can bribe me with expensive champagne."

John reached into the front pocket of his robe and pulled out her favorite vibrator.

"How about Buzz then?"

"That's not good enough."

"Then what can I do?"

"Take your robe off."

CHAPTER NINETEEN

TRUE CONFESSIONS

Maggie was working on another commission in her loft, when the phone rang. She turned down her music.

"Miss O'Reilly, I'm Emily Brown. My parents purchased your grandparent's home back in 1993. I recently inherited it from them. In the process of my renovations, I found three Banker's Boxes in a closet we discovered behind a bookcase in the library. I looked inside and found letters and documents that you may want to go through."

"I have to go to Tuscaloosa this Wednesday; could I come by on my way?"

"Sure. Call me ahead of time so I can meet you there. "

Maggie was saddened when she saw her grandparents' house totally gutted. Walking back to where her grandmother's kitchen once was brought back memories of Bessie baking Toll House cookies.

Maggie arrived at Ron's place just in time for cocktails. It had been almost a year since their last visit. Maggie noticed that Ron was getting a little pudgy, which was so unlike him. After a dinner of veal chops, they took their wine into the living room.

"You're such a wonderful cook. You could make someone a great husband, speaking of, are you still seeing that professor you told me about?"

"Yes. She is in Atlanta at a conference. She's moving in with me in two weeks."

"It's gotten that serious? How wonderful for you. I noticed you removed the nude painting you did of me."

"Yes, Margaret asked me to take it down. I want you to have it."

"I'll treasure it."

Saturday morning Maggie started sorting through the three Banker's Boxes. She smiled to herself as she found one box filled with coloring book pictures and handmade cards she had colored and given to her grandmother. At a young age, her art skills were evident; she especially enjoyed drawing animals and flowers. She found the first self-portrait she had done in kindergarten. She might frame it and jokingly give it to John.

The second Banker's Box was filled with letters and cards between Maggie's Grandparents. Her grandfather, Jackson Beauregard, served in a Mobile Army Surgical Hospital during the Korean War. She opened a bottle of wine and read each of their love letters aloud and yearned for the special love they shared. She saved the final box until the next morning. Influenced by the love letters she had read, she texted John.

"It seems time stands still when you are away, yet when we are finally together time is like a blink of the eye. I can't wait until we get reacquainted at the beach... in the few stolen moments we can find."

The next morning she read his reply. *"Once I get this new office opened, I will have more time to be with you. I can't wait to make love to you in your Mermaid Grotto."*

She started on the final Banker's Box filled with past tax returns and other documents which didn't interest her. Around noon she was about ready to trash everything in the file when she came across a folder titled *Divorce Settlement*.

Maggie thought *whose divorce?* She opened the file and saw a copy of her parents' divorce decree with other documents attached and several photographs. Maggie first looked at the photographs which were of her mother having oral sex with some man with blond hair, obviously not her auburn-haired dad. Another photo showed Wanda with the same guy and another woman who was giving Wanda oral sex as Blondie was penetrating mystery woman from behind.

There was a copy of a cashiers check for $750,000 payable to James O'Reilly.

As Maggie rummaged through the remaining paperwork, she completed the puzzle. Her father had been paid hush money by her grandparents not to expose their daughter, Wanda, in a scandalous divorce. Maggie shook her head in disbelief and said, "Damn. So not to tarnish the Beauregard family image. And here I've always blamed my father for their divorce."

Maggie snapped a picture of it with her phone and attached it to an email to her father.

"After all these years, why did you not tell me the truth? As a child I believed when you moved far away, you didn't love us anymore."

Within a minute, her father called her to tell his side of the story.

"Some scumbag reporter blackmailed your Grandparents with the pictures you found. Your mother was having an affair with a State Senator. Ironically, your Grandfather had donated generously to the Senator's election campaign. They paid the reporter $100,000 in hush money and paid me $750,000 to agree to be the guilty party in the divorce and to move at least 1,000 miles away. I ended up moving to New Mexico to work for my uncle's plumbing company."

Maggie and Mary were sharing an order of coconut shrimp and drinking Bushwackers at Flora-Bama when Mary said, "Is John coming to see you Mardi Gras week?"

"No, our plans changed. I have to go to New York while Matthew's mother has surgery. John is coming to see me there."

"You've been dating him for a while now. Have ya'll talked about getting married?"

"In a roundabout way, I guess. It's complicated, working on opposite coasts."

"Well, couldn't you paint your commissions in San Francisco and then commute to New York like you already do?"

"Mary, he hasn't proposed to me."

John had just received the lab results from his doctor's office. During his previous Hong Kong trip in December, he had gone out for Friday night cocktails with Ted, a fraternity brother who practiced international law in Hong Kong. The bar was located in the pulsating red-light district of Wan Chai, an area that John had always avoided. When he had hooked up in the past, he had always used high-class escort services. But that was before he had met Maggie, and he had no intentions of being unfaithful to her; that same day he had bought her a diamond engagement ring at the Cartier store. While sitting at the bar, he showed the ring to Ted. A lithe Asian young woman came over and started hitting on them both. John was ready to go back to his hotel room, but Ted bought a round of drinks for the three of them and then wandered off to pursue a prostitute he had hired several times before. John started feeling dizzy, and the woman offered to escort him to a cab so he could go back to his hotel.

The next thing John remembered, it was 10 a.m. on Saturday, and he woke up naked lying on his hotel bed. He had been robbed of all his clothes, his cell phone, wallet, and the ring. His return flight was scheduled the next afternoon. Fortunately he had put his passport and ticket in the room safe. The hotel found John's cell phone in the elevator. Ted came over to the hotel, loaned him clothes to wear and one thousand dollars. Ted told John that the woman at the bar must have spiked his drink with Rohypnol.

John's hands were trembling as he waited for Maggie to answer her phone. His voice quivered when he spoke. "Maggie, can you talk?"

"You don't sound good, what's wrong?

"Please forgive me when I tell you this. You need to see your doctor. I have an STD."

"I don't understand. I'm screened annually; you're my only partner since my last screening."

"It's not what you think."

"Have you been with someone?"

"My previous trip to Hong Kong, I went to a bar with a friend, and I can't remember what happened. We think someone slipped me Rohypnol."

"Why didn't you tell me this before I slept with you at the Ritz?"

"I believed I'd only been robbed."

"You still should have confided in me. It's not like someone just picked your pocket. Forget about coming to see me in New York."

The following afternoon Maggie left the doctor's office with a prescription to take Doxycycline twice a day for seven days. Tomorrow she would return to New York before Matthew left for Chicago to be with his mom for her second knee replacement surgery. She was glad she would have a reason to pull herself together; she had been tempted to cut again.

CHAPTER TWENTY

A GHOST FROM THE PAST

A snowstorm had cut down on the gallery's foot traffic. Maggie let Connie leave early. The storm was not expected to let up until the next afternoon; people were being advised to avoid getting out unless absolutely necessary. Maggie had already made plans not to open the gallery the next day. The door buzzer went off and she thought, *who on earth is out in this weather?* As she walked into the main gallery, she was stunned to see a ghost from her past, an attractive ghost, with a charming familiar smile.

Her heart rate increased as she remembered the first time she met him at Café 290, a jazz club she frequented in Atlanta. A co-worker, Maria, encouraged her to flirt with him at the bar. He was the sexiest man Maggie had ever seen and ended up in his hotel room for the next forty-eight hours.

"Sean?"

"Hi, Mags. I hoped you might be here. I saw Matthew this weekend in Chicago. He told me you were minding the gallery while he takes care of his mom."

"What brings you to New York?"

"Unfinished business with you."

"Our business is finished; I've told you this before."

"You've never listened to my side of the story. I never intended to do you any harm."

"Let's not go there."

"Please, listen to me. That's all I'm asking, and then I will never bother you again."

"Alright… let me close up here, and we can talk."

"How about we go to Da Nico and get a pizza?"

"You know my weakness for pizza."

Maggie had not been back to Da Nico since Sean had taken her there for her twenty-seventh birthday. In fact, she had avoided almost any place they had been together.

Sean ordered a bottle of the Tumalolo-Chianti and their favorite pizza, Pizza Quatro Stagioni. They chatted like old friends while they drank wine and ate pizza.

"National Geographic offered me an editorial position. I turned it down since I prefer photojournalism. You know how I love to travel. I'm not ready to give it up, so I've started freelancing. Today I had a lunch meeting with *The Times* to discuss an assignment they want me to do in Syria."

"That sounds dangerous."

"It pays well. I told them I would let them know by Monday. I get to call my own shots now. Don't you remember how difficult it was for us to plan a vacation because of the conflicts with my work?"

"I got to go with you on several of your assignments, which wasn't so bad."

"Except when you got malaria in Madagascar."

"That was horrible."

"What about you; are you still painting erotic self-portraits?"

"I've changed my focus; I'm painting portraits of cancer survivors."

"That sounds fulfilling."

"I love my work. Matthew told me you divorced."

"Amy finally agreed to an annulment, oddly right after you and I broke up. Ray, this guy she was having an affair with, divorced his wife and ended up marrying Amy. I didn't know if the baby she lost was mine or Ray's."

"I'm confused. All I knew was that you had a son with her."

"Not true. I had a one-night stand with Amy, and she claimed I'd gotten her pregnant. I was pressured to do the honorable thing and marry her. During this same time, my sister, Sara, who was fifteen, became pregnant, and her baby was due the same week as Amy's. To protect Sara's reputation, I convinced Amy we should adopt Sara's son, Michael, and pretend we had twins. Unfortunately, Amy's baby was stillborn. She became depressed and resentful of both Michael and me, and she moved out. A devoted Catholic, she refused to get a divorce. I finally convinced her we should get an annulment."

Maggie couldn't believe what she had just heard. "This sounds like a soap opera; what happened to Michael?"

"With my financial support, my mother and Sara have been raising him. We just told Michael that Sara is his real mother, and I'm his uncle."

"I'm afraid I was misled by what Matthew told me."

"Please don't blame Matthew. He didn't find out the truth until I saw him this week."

She was having an anxiety attack. "Can we get out of here? I need some fresh air."

They walked for several blocks in silence. At a loss for words, she couldn't even label her emotions. She wanted to run away. Not knowing this truth had changed everything in her life, and now knowing the truth was not any better.

Maggie was oblivious to how bitterly cold it was. The wind had picked up, and Sean realized it was too cold to continue walking. He stopped a taxi and told Maggie, "You're freezing. Get in this taxi. Where are you staying?"

"At Matthew's."

He walked her to Matthew's apartment door, and she trembled as she tried to unlock it.

"Give me your key."

As he opened her door, he asked, "Are you going to be okay?"

He ushered her inside and held her tightly to his chest. "Hey, calm down; everything is fine."

"I was wrong to have treated you that way. What a beautiful thing you did for your sister."

"Don't blame yourself. I didn't like hiding this secret from you. You're all wet; go change while I find us something to drink."

Maggie changed into her red cashmere robe and wrapped her wet hair in a towel. Sean brought her a Sambuca and sat down next to her on the sofa.

"Mags, I had no idea you stopped seeing me because Matthew told you I had a son. I made a vow to my sister I would never reveal the truth until she was ready. I couldn't tell you."

"Why did you think I stopped seeing you?"

"I've been agonizing over that for years. Hiding the truth and Amy's refusal to get a divorce caused me to start using cocaine more. I became more possessive of you. I didn't want you out of my sight. I was afraid you would find a better lover. I guess I loved you too much. I've since gone through a drug rehab program and have been drug-free for eighteen months. I've caused you enough anguish. I'll leave."

"I don't want to be alone. You can stay in Matthew's room. I'm going to get ready for bed."

When she returned, she found Sean and Guido lying on the sofa. Sean had brought a pillow and blanket from Matthew's room and was under the blanket nude with the cat lying on top of his feet.

"Guido makes a great foot warmer. If you don't mind, I would rather sleep here on the sofa. No telling who Matthew has had in his bed."

Maggie went over and sat on the edge of the sofa running her fingers through his wavy raven hair. "You have the most beautiful hair."

"Go get your comb and pony tail holder so I can comb and braid your hair."

One of their pre-mating rituals was for Sean to comb her hair and braid it in a low ponytail. As he combed and braided her hair, she recalled how he would tug on her braid while he took her from behind.

When he finished, she asked, "Can I lie with you for awhile?"

Maggie turned off the overhead light and dropped her robe to the floor. Sean lifted the blanket, and she slipped under next to him. He placed his arms around her waist breathing in her lavender scent.

He said, "You're still shaking. Are you warm enough?"

"You're warming me up."

"I'm so sorry you were hurt and confused by this terrible misunderstanding. Will you give me a second chance?"

"I don't know. I need some time to sort this all out. A lot about me has changed since we were together."

Maggie turned to face him. She peered into his hazel eyes searching for an answer to her dilemma. *Why am I feeling this old familiar lust inside me?*

Sean lifted his head so that their lips were almost touching. Instinctively, she parted her mouth, and he lightly bit her lower lip. She breathed in his familiar scent, Gucci *Guilty Black*, she thought how appropriate the name. He started kissing her, and she knew she had to fight the urge.

Pulling away, she said, "We must stop. I'm too confused right now." She rolled over on her side.

Sean whispered in her ear "I warn you, you'll be begging me soon. I love you."

Maggie did not hesitate when she replied, "I love you too."

The next morning she woke up feeling the warmth of her former lover against her back. *What am I going to do?* His white lie had turned her life upside down. Now she knew the truth at last. He did a noble thing for his sister and his family.

Sorting through this mess made Maggie a nervous wreck. She got up from the sofa and put on her robe. As she checked her phone, she thought John was probably in some remote Asian area without cell service. Why did she feel so guilty? He had slept with a prostitute in Hong Kong. She had only slept nude with her former boyfriend; no bodily fluids were exchanged.

She made a pot of French roast coffee. Guido rubbed against her ankles; she gave him his morning Tender Vittles.

Commando style, Sean walked into the kitchen. Hugging her from behind rekindled those familiar feelings she had tried to block out. She had the urge to relinquish her control over to him again.

"Will you please put your pants on; I need to talk seriously to you."

He returned wearing a pair of Matthew's sweatpants. She could see his hard erection stretching the fabric. The urge to make love to him overwhelmed her. He always had these strong erections first thing in the morning that many times would last over an hour. Morning sex was always the best with him.

Maggie had made him a mug of coffee, black with a teaspoon of sugar, just the way he liked it. He sat down on the sofa next to her.

Her hand was shaking as she picked up her mug. "A lot has happened since we were together."

"I can tell by your tattoo and your hair removal you weren't idle."

Maggie raised her right eyebrow and said, "Can I continue?"

"Mags, I'm teasing you."

"I'm seeing someone."

"Is it serious; do you love him?"

Maggie felt as though she were on trial in a courtroom. "I'm not sure anymore. He betrayed me. He gave me an STD he picked up during a business trip to Hong Kong. He told me this prostitute had drugged him."

"And you believe such bullshit. I doubt seriously that it was nonconsensual. When they drug their victims, they don't usually have sex; they just rob them. I did an article on the Wan Chai Sex Industry. I believe no man can resist the erotic temptation that abounds in their districts. I certainly couldn't. It's like taking a diabetic to a candy shop; how could they resist cheating?"

Maggie shook her head, "I don't know what to believe anymore."

"Believe in me. Give me a chance to prove to you that I love you. I don't want to lose you again. I'm not going to take no for an answer. Face it, you require a special man to meet your sexual needs."

Maggie stood up and walked over to the window. "It looks like we're snowed in."

Sean walked over and embraced her from behind. "Would you like me to cook you breakfast?"

"I don't have anything for you to cook."

"There's a market just a block away; I can walk there and get a few things."

"Let me get dressed, and I'll go with you."

Maggie prepared Bloody Marys. "Every year for Christmas I ship a case of this Whiskey Willy Bloody Mary mix to Matthew. It's made in Orange Beach."

Sean tasted it. "It's spicy, just like you. Now if you will get two plates out and stack the English muffins and Canadian bacon on them, I'll have our poached eggs ready in a second. I've got the Hollandaise sauce finished."

"You always make the best Eggs Benedict!"

"Let's sit down and eat before it gets cold."

As they washed the dishes, Maggie said, "What can we do today?"

"Do you want me to spend the day with you?"

"What would you do otherwise?"

"I don't have to go back to Chicago until Friday. Why don't I go back to my hotel and shower, change my clothes, and pick up something to cook for dinner? We can watch one of Matthew's DVDs."

"Have you seen *The Girl with the Dragon Tattoo*? I gave it to him for Christmas."

"No, but I saw the girl with a butterfly tattoo."

"That's not funny."

"I couldn't resist."

"Why don't you check out of your hotel and stay here?"

The afternoon they shared brought back many wonderful memories Maggie had tried to forget. She had forgotten how charming and romantic he could be. Sean was the flamboyant type while John was the complete opposite, much more restrained.

After the movie, Sean prepared linguini with clam sauce. He had picked up a bottle of Santa Margherita Pinot Grigio at the market. They dined by candlelight at the small kitchen table, a tradition they had shared when they lived together in Chicago.

"Sean, you remembered how much I love this wine."

"It's pairs well with the brininess of the clams. Would you like to take our wine into the living room and listen to some music? Matthew has an incredible collection of 70's music."

Sean searched through Matthew's hundreds of CDs. "Here's one I know you'll like." The music started, and it was Carol King's *I Feel the Earth Move*. "Remember how this was our theme song."

When she lived with Sean, she would dance around and sing along with this album. When *So Far Away* played, Sean asked her to dance with him. As they slow danced, Maggie said, "I forgot what a good dancer you are."

Maggie became melancholy when the next song, *It's Too Late* started playing.

"Mags, it's never too late." She could not refuse his kiss. His kisses were like an addictive drug to her. Despite the numerous times he had wronged her, she always surrendered to him when he kissed her like this.

"Mags, I want to ask you a serious question and I want an honest answer. Before Matthew told you I had a son, would you have married me?"

"I would have done anything you wanted me to do."

"We've already lost too much time apart; I want to marry you and start a family."

185

Sean unzipped her fleece hoodie, exposing her breasts. He leaned down and sucked each nipple intensively. It pleased him that she was still so responsive to his stimulation; he had conditioned her like Pavlov did with his dogs. Scooping her up, he carried her to the guest bedroom.

Maggie always enjoyed watching him undress. His half-Irish and half-Italian heritage had blessed him with his exotic good looks. As an avid amateur boxer, his body was ripped. He knew once he made love to her, she would be totally his again. His cock was ready. As she reached out to stroke him, he pushed her down on the bed. With his dominant left hand, he pinned her hands above her head. His right hand slipped under the waistband of her leggings and rubbed against her bare pelvis.

"What made you decide to get rid of your hair?"

"I got a wild hair, no pun intended."

"I think I might like you this way; I just need to get used to it."

His fingers found her G-Spot. After a shuddering climax, he sucked her dry, then kissed her deeply.

"You've never had a G-Spot climax with me before."

Maggie's hand grasped his cock as she begged, "I want you."

"I told you, you would be begging for this. Get on your hands and knees to the side of the bed."

Her cries of erotic passion brought out a rage inside him. His large bare hand marked her buttocks, pushing her to the point of no return.

"That's a good girl. Release yourself to me. Get it all out!"

Maggie sounded like a wild animal being broken in, as she screamed, "Sean...please...please...forgive me."

As Sean released himself, he grunted, "You're forgiven."

The last thing Maggie wanted to do was to get out of the warm bed. While the coffee brewed, she sent Connie an email saying she would not be at the gallery. She had not checked her inbox for several days. John had sent a message on Monday. She hesitated before she opened it.

"Maggie I'm sorry I screwed up. Please give me a second chance. I realize how much I love you. John."

This was the first time John had ever directly communicated his love for her. Maggie shook her head side to side. *What I have done is even worse than what John did to me. I had sex with my former lover. Why do I still have this ache inside me?*

Her bewildered thoughts were interrupted when Sean suddenly walked in.

"You look troubled?"

"I'm fine." She immediately hit delete. *Wouldn't it be nice if life had a delete button you could push to get rid of things you wish you had never done?*

"Sorry, I had to contact Connie and let her know I won't be coming in today. I just made some coffee; would you like me to get you some?"

"You stay there; I'll get some. Would you like a cup? You like it with a splash of half and half right?'

"Please."

After Sean poured their coffee, he sat down next to Maggie on the sofa.

"I have something for you."

He reached into the pocket of his sweatpants, pulled out a small pink velvet box, and handed it to her. Inside the box she found a gold Claddagh ring. The Claddagh's distinctive design featured two hands clasping a heart that was surmounted by a crown.

"My Irish grandfather gave this to my grandmother as an engagement ring over seventy years ago. My grandmother passed it on to me before she died. She told me it was time for me to find a bride and raise a family. I know it's not a traditional

187

engagement ring, but it has a special meaning-- the heart stands for love, the hands stand for friendship, and the crown stands for loyalty."

"How lovely."

"When you become engaged you wear it on your left hand facing outward and then when you become married you face it inward. Let's see if it fits you."

Maggie shook her head, "Sean, It's too soon."

"Then wear it on your right hand with the heart facing inward which means someone has captured your heart."

Maggie took the ring and started to slide it on her right ring finger; she stopped and handed it back to Sean.

She held out her left hand and said, "I think it will look much nicer on this hand."

Sean slid it on her left ring finger. It was a perfect fit. "Mags, you've made me so happy. Let's not wait. Let's get married now. I won't go to Syria."

"No. Go on your trip. I have two painting commissions I have to finish. And I know this might sound silly, but I'd like to have a nice wedding."

They spent the rest of the day making love and planning their future together. Sean's paternal grandparents had gotten married in a small palazzo in Pantelleria, Italy. Sean's Aunt Sophia had inherited the palazzo and converted it into an inn. Sean called his Aunt and asked if they could get married there. Luckily, she had just gotten a cancellation, and the first weekend in June was available.

After an afternoon meeting at the tax accountant's office, Maggie returned to Matthew's. She already missed Sean, who had left that morning. Matthew had left a message on her cell phone to call him.

"Hi, Matthew, how is Joyce doing?"

"You know my mom; she hates being limited in what she can do. Although, I must say, she enjoys having me wait on her hand and foot."

"I'm sure you're spoiling her."

"Enough about my mom. Connie told me you didn't go into the gallery yesterday. Are you okay?"

"Sean came to see me. He told me the truth about Amy and Michael."

"I'm sorry you're just finding this out. I didn't find out myself until last weekend. He told me not to say anything to you about it."

"I want you to be the first to know; we're engaged."

"You and John?"

"No, Sean and me."

"Have you gone insane? You can't be serious?"

"We're getting married the first weekend in June at your Aunt's palazzo in Pantelleria, Italy. We both want you to be the best man."

"Why are you in such a rush to get married?"

"We compromised. Sean wanted to get married immediately. He doesn't want to wait any longer since we've been already separated for too long."

"If you will recall, you started dating Sean on the rebound shortly after your divorce from that SOD you married. And Sean, I recall, was also recently separated from Amy then."

"Please don't lecture me. I want your support as my friend."

"As your friend, I can't stand by and watch you make perhaps the biggest mistake of your life. And what about John? Your relationship with him seems really good. And Maggie, John respects you, something I don't think Sean is capable of."

"John has not been a saint. He gave me an STD."

"You're kidding?"

"Nope. Instead of bringing me jade jewelry from Hong Kong, he brought me The Clam."

"Maggie, I'm curious; did you give Sean any money when he came to see you?"

Maggie thought that it was an odd question to ask her. "I gave him some money to wire to his Aunt so she can help us make the wedding arrangements. Why did you want to know this?"

"I would rather talk about this when I see you in person next week."

CHAPTER TWENTY-ONE

MATTHEW'S ACCOUNT

"Mary, this is Matthew. Are you where you can talk in private?"

"Yes, Maggie is taking a shower. What's up?"

"I have some disturbing news. I'm so glad you're staying with Maggie. I just found out Sean was killed in Syria yesterday."

"Oh, how horrible. Maggie is going to be really upset. What should I do?"

"Don't let her listen to the news. They've been reporting on it. I'm leaving now to go to the airport and will be there in the morning to tell her myself."

"What about your mother?"

"My aunt is coming to take my place. I have to go now. I'll see you in the morning."

Maggie fainted when Matthew told her the news. When she regained consciousness, she was frightened and disoriented. Although she recognized Mary, she didn't know who Matthew was. She kept asking them to take her to her apartment in Atlanta. Mary called her uncle who was Maggie's psychiatrist in Gulf Shores, and he called Dr. Roberts, a classmate of his in Santa Rosa, California who ran a specialized memory clinic. Dr. Roberts calmed Maggie down on the phone and persuaded her to be at his clinic on Monday. Maggie flew with Mary to Santa Rosa the next day.

191

Monday morning, Matthew received a call from Dr. Roberts. "Matthew this is Dr. Roberts. I appreciate you agreeing to talk to me. I'll be meeting with Maggie in an hour. Mary told me that you're one of Maggie's closest friend. Could you give me a little background on your relationship with her?"

"I first met her when she started dating Sean."

"So Sean was your friend?"

"My cousin. We grew up together in Chicago. We were quite close. I was the godfather of Michael."

"Mary told me that Michael was Sean's sister's son."

"Yes. Sean had everyone fooled including me. He just told me that truth the last time I was with him."

"Can you tell me what you know about Sean and Maggie's relationship?"

"Shortly after Sean separated from Amy, he met Maggie. Sean worked as a photojournalist for National Geographic Magazine at that time and traveled all over the world. Maggie had moved to Atlanta after her divorce. She was working for a bank. They met at a jazz club while he was on an assignment in Atlanta. They were in a long-distance relationship for almost a year before Sean convinced her to come live with him. Maggie quit her job and moved to Chicago."

"Tell me more about their relationship."

"Sean was possessive of her. When he went on an assignment, he would take her with him, and when he couldn't, he would monitor her every move. She was almost like his prisoner."

"If he was possessive of Maggie, how did you become friends with her?"

"Sean started taking these erotic pictures of her, and she started painting from them. I saw her paintings in Sean's apartment and was blown away by her unique style. At that time, I had recently stopped my modeling career and was managing an art gallery in New York. I asked Maggie if she would like to do an exhibit there. With Sean's permission, she eventually agreed.

"During the night of the opening exhibit, Sean was on an assignment out of the country. I took Maggie out afterwards to celebrate. We both had too much champagne, and I brought up Michael. Maggie was shocked. She knew Sean was in the process of getting a divorce from Amy, but she didn't know about Michael. Selfishly that night, I encouraged her to leave him."

"Why do you mean by selfishly?"

"I was attracted to her; she deserved better than Sean."

"What happened then?"

"The next day, we flew to Chicago. She wanted to move back to Gulf Shores where her family once had a beach house that had been destroyed by Hurricane Ivan. I helped her move into an apartment near the beach where she lived while she built a new cottage on her family's beachfront property. During this time, we would visit one another and we became friends with benefits. Later we become partners in a new business, Maggie came up with the concept of The Launch gallery."

"How did Sean react to Maggie leaving him?"

"He was livid, to put it mildly. She never told him why she left him which made it worse. For about a year he begged her to come back. He finally stopped when he found a younger replacement for her."

"Why do you think he went to New York to make amends and propose to her?"

"While staying with my mother in Chicago, I saw Sean. He asked me about Maggie. I told him that she'd started dating again which made him jealous. I told him he'd blown his chance by hiding the fact he had a son from her. That's when Sean told me the truth about Michael being his nephew and not his son.

"I hate to say this about my cousin, but he has always been an opportunist. His recreational habits, including both drugs and gambling, caused him to live well above his means. He asked me if I could loan him some money to pay off a gambling debt. He told me he was getting a new freelance job and wouldn't get paid until he completed the assignment and he could pay me back then."

"So what are you alluding to?"

"Guess who has lots of money?"

"Maggie."

"I talked to Maggie on the phone, and she told me about her sudden engagement with Sean. She had also given him some money to use for their wedding arrangements. I was planning on telling her about my prior conversation with Sean when I returned to New York. I now regret I didn't tell her then over the phone. Unfortunately, my next conversation with her was telling her the tragic news."

"Mary mentioned Maggie was also involved in another relationship with a guy named John. Can you tell me about their relationship?"

"I'm was convinced Maggie had fallen in love with John and that he loves her. However, he recently passed on an STD to her. He claims while on his business trip to Hong Kong, a woman put a roofie in his drink. He doesn't remember anything that happened, he believed he had just been robbed."

"Rohypnol can cause complete amnesia, especially when digested with alcohol. How did Maggie and John meet?"

"He lives in San Francisco. She met him last year at the Atlanta Airport. In some respects, he's somewhat like Sean."

"In what ways?"

"He's an excellent photographer and like Sean did, he took nude pictures of her."

"Interesting. Any other things they have in common?"

"They both like to play a little rough with her."

"What do you mean?"

"BDSM stuff."

"Maggie told you this?"

"Remember, I also had a short fling with her. I knew first hand she enjoyed being dominated."

"Was there ever any physical abuse?"

"She never came out and told me so, but I was suspicious. Sean would give her drugs sometimes."

"What kind of drugs?"

"Coke and Molly. I dropped by one night, and Sean offered to share her with me. He'd tied her to his Saint Andrews Cross. He was extremely high, and he told me she was acting like a whore. I told Sean he needed to untie her and get some rest. He told me to mind my own business and leave."

"Did Maggie ever say anything about Sean hurting her?"

"After they broke up, I asked her about that night. She told me Sean liked for her to dress up in this promiscuous outfit he'd bought her and go to a bar so he could watch guys hit on her. That particular night, he gave her a Molly to take before they went out. At the bar, this guy who she was dancing with started feeling her up under her skirt. Sean became enraged, took her home, drugged her more, and tied her to the cross. She doesn't remember me coming over or anything else that happened that night."

"How about John; does he act that abusive towards her?"

"I don't think so. Maggie has never said anything. I know he doesn't abuse drugs like Sean does."

"Can you think of anything else that might be helpful?"

"I swore to Maggie, not to tell anyone about her first lover, but under the circumstances, I think it might be pertinent. When Maggie was six, her parent's divorced. After the divorce, her mom, Wanda, was involved with several men, mostly quite younger than her. There was a young writer named, Christopher, who spent several summers with them at their beach house. When Maggie was eighteen, he became her first lover. He insisted that she save her virginity until she entered college and went on birth control. But they did everything else. One night they were left alone, and they had anal sex for the first time. The next day Maggie's mother discovered they'd slept together. Wanda was a vindictive bitch. She made Maggie watch as she dominated Christopher."

"What exactly did she do?"

"It gets barbaric here. Wanda whipped Christopher with a riding crop then gave him a blowjob and directed his cum all over Maggie's face. I felt so sad when Maggie told me she would rather have been raped than to have witnessed what her mother did to Christopher. She also admitted, she started cutting herself after that to manage the pain she felt."

"Interesting that her mother wanted to prove to Maggie that she had the ultimate control over him."

"Maggie told me that when Hurricane Ivan destroyed the beach house, she went to inspect the damage. Oddly, she found only one thing left, a bronze mermaid statue that Christopher had given to her for her fifteenth birthday. She believed her mother had gotten rid of it. Evidently her mother had hidden it somewhere in the beach house all these years. Maggie keeps this statue on her coffee table. I once asked her why she kept the statute out; did she still have feelings for him? She looked me straight in the eye and said, "Matthew, how could I not?" I didn't want to pry any further."

"It's quite ironic that the only thing that survived the storm was the gift from her first lover. Has she ever been in contact with him again?"

"He recently published a book titled, *My Innocent Mermaid*, which is loosely based on their relationship. Maggie went to one of his book signing events. He attempted to hook back up with her, but she turned him down."

CHAPTER TWENTY-TWO

JOHN'S ACCOUNT

Damn it; why doesn't Maggie answer her phone. I'm sure she knows I'm back now. She's ignoring my emails. Maybe she isn't back from New York. I've got to convince her to give me a second chance, to explain what happened. I've had no desire to be with any other woman since the day I met her. I'll try calling Matthew.

"Matthew, this is John."

"You're back from your trip already?"

"I came in early yesterday morning. I desperately need to talk to Maggie; is she there? She won't answer her cell phone or emails."

"When you give someone an STD, they're entitled to get angry."

"I was drugged, Matthew."

Matthew hesitated before he responded, "John, I'll give you the benefit of the doubt. I have some terrible news. Maggie is not doing well."

"What do you mean?"

"She has dissociative amnesia; can't remember anything that happened these last seven years."

"How the hell did this happen?"

"Maggie has had to deal with a lot of stress in her life. Sharon's death was extremely traumatic. While you were away she experienced another traumatic experience, that caused a domino effect on her brain."

"What happened?"

"I'm pretty sure she told you she once lived with this guy named Sean."

"I know that. He was nothing but a scumbag. He hid from her that he had a son."

"What Maggie didn't know was it wasn't his son, it was his younger sister's illegitimate son. He was trying to protect his sister's reputation."

Matthew proceeded to tell John what he knew about Maggie and Sean's relationship.

Matthew said, "I think in a state of confusion Maggie felt obligated to give Sean a second chance."

John couldn't believe what he was hearing. "A second chance? And all this has happened since I've been away. Matthew, there has got to be more to this insane story."

"I'm afraid there is. They got engaged, but Mary told me Maggie was questioning her quick decision and thinking of postponing the engagement."

"He didn't waste any time I can see. He has obviously taken advantage of her vulnerability."

"I think he was after her money; he was over his head in debt."

"And she was an easy target for him. But why does she have this amnesia?"

"I know you're mad, John, but after they got engaged a terrible thing happened. Did you hear about the journalist that was recently killed by Syrian security forces?"

"It was all over the news. He was there filming a documentary about Syrians fleeing the country for Turkey. Oh, my God, wait his name was Sean."

"Maggie went into shock when I told her what happened, which caused her to block her memory these last seven years. She doesn't remember anything since she first met Sean."

"I've heard of this type of amnesia before. It's due to psychological triggers rather than physiological causes."

"John, she doesn't remember anyone she has met since that time. She doesn't know that I'm her business partner, or for that matter, that she has a business. She doesn't know who you are either. She can only recall being recently divorced, her college years and any time before that."

"Where is she now?"

"She's at a residency program that specializes in memory disorders. It's not too far from you in Santa Rosa, California. Mary's father who is a psychiatrist, pulled some strings to get Maggie in despite a long waiting list. The Santa Rosa doctor was intrigued by the complexity of Maggie's case."

"That's reassuring. What's the prognosis that she'll regain her memory?"

"They don't know yet. Could be days, weeks, months, or even years. The memories still exist, but are deeply buried in her mind and for now cannot be recalled."

John said, "I want to see her."

"You have to get permission from her doctor. I'll be glad to send you his name and contact information."

"Send it to me."

I'm greatly upset by what has happened. I wish I could just get mad at the whole thing and blame Sean for taking Maggie away from me. And then how he made her feel obligated to take him back since he did such a noble thing to protect his little sister. All he really wanted was her inheritance. Oh, Maggie O', why did you fall for his poisonous bait? It's because I screwed up in Hong Kong. I should have never gone with Ted to that bar that night."

"Thank you for meeting with me, Dr. Roberts. As I told you on the phone, Maggie and I have been in a close relationship since January of last year."

"If that is the case, why do you think she became engaged to Sean?"

"I'm just as puzzled as you are. Maggie told me a lot about her past relationship with Sean. He was controlling and manipulative of her during their tempestuous relationship."

"Did he ever hurt her?"

"They had a sort of a loose BDSM relationship."

"As far as 'loose', what do you mean by that?"

"Dominants are never supposed to punish their subordinates when they are angry."

"Did he violate this rule?"

"She told me he went past her limits, which scared her."

"I was told he also gave her drugs."

"Yes, ecstasy and cocaine. She would have trouble remembering what had happened. There is something else I have to tell you. Maggie was livid at me for passing on an STD. A prostitute in Hong Kong drugged me, raped me, and robbed me. A friend who was with me at the bar saw her a week ago and contacted the police. She had slipped Rohypnol in another businessman's drink that night as well. They arrested her. I have a copy of the police report. I would never do anything to hurt Maggie; please, believe me. Dr. Roberts, I want to see her."

"Could you come tomorrow?"

John said, "Just let me know the time."

"We want to observe her as she meets people from her past. We'll be watching you through a security camera."

John felt anxious as he was driving to see Maggie. He stopped at a market and picked up a bunch of sunflowers for her. When he arrived, he was asked to wait in the reception area. Dr. Roberts came out to greet him.

"I think the timing of your visit is good. Maggie is getting quite annoyed and restless here. Hopefully, your visit will encourage her."

John said, "Yes, she can be quite feisty."

He followed Dr. Roberts to a small conference room where Maggie was sitting with her back to him. He couldn't help but call out, "Maggie."

She turned her chair around and smiled at him. "Hi, am I supposed to know you?"

Dr. Roberts quickly interjected, "Maggie, this is John. He's a friend of yours. He's from San Francisco and wanted to come by and see you today."

Maggie said, "How nice. My grandparents took me to San Francisco when I was little. I liked the Chocolate Factory there."

John replied, "Yes, it's at Ghirardelli Square."

Dr. Roberts said, "If you'll excuse me, I have something I need to do. I'll be back a little later."

Maggie said, "Those are beautiful sunflowers that you have."

John felt this awkward boyish nervousness as he handed them to her. "They're for you."

Maggie smiled again. "For me? Thank you!"

"What do you like to do?"

"I like to draw. While I ended up majoring in finance to please my mother, I also majored in art, my real passion."

"Where did you graduate from?"

"Alabama."

"Roll Tide. Do you like going to the beach?"

"We used to have a beach house in Gulf Shores, but it was washed away during Hurricane Ivan. I felt a special part of my life was washed away. You see, I spent almost every summer there while I was growing up. I still have these vivid memories of growing up there. Years later when my mother wasn't feeling well, we couldn't decide whether to rebuild it or sell the lot. I don't know what happened. They told me my mother died of cancer. I hope we didn't get rid of the beach property. Do you perhaps know what happened?"

"I'm sorry about your mother. Yes, I do know about the beach property; you built a beautiful cottage where the old house once stood."

"I did? That makes me happy."

"I'm glad."

Maggie started blushing at John like she did when they first met at the airport. She raised her right eyebrow and asked, "Why are you staring at me that way?"

"Your eyes are almost the color of your sweater."

"I'm sorry I didn't have a chance to wear something nice. My friend Mary let me borrow her sweater. They won't allow me to wear most of my clothes."

John asked, "Why is that?"

"They said the clothes I brought are much too risqué since men also stay here. So they gave me these scrubs to wear."

"I must say, you look nice in them."

"Thank you. And I like your red Burberry tie."

John thought it was interesting that she recognized it was a Burberry. He saw his Maggie begging to come out when she just flirted with him. He was so tempted to grab her and kiss her.

Dr. Roberts came back in. "Maggie, it's time for you to leave now. You need to get ready for the yoga class."

"Do I have to? I'm enjoying talking to John."

Dr. Roberts said, "He'll come back and visit you another time."

Maggie looked directly into John's eyes. "John, please say you will."

"I promise you, Maggie."

"And thank you for the sunflowers; they're my favorite flower."

It seemed like the longest drive back home for John. He convinced Dr. Roberts to let him visit again. Dr. Roberts told John he would be there Sunday afternoon and could come then.

On his second visit, John brought several gifts for Maggie. Dr. Roberts said, "John, I'm okay with you giving her the Ghirardelli candy and the sketchbook/pencil set, but she can't have the scarf for safety reasons."

John replied, "You mean she might hang herself with it?"

"There is always a risk. Freudian psychology suggests that dissociative amnesia is an act of self-preservation during which the alternative might be overwhelming anxiety or even suicide."

"She left this houndstooth scarf at my place. It was her favorite, and I thought it might help her remember."

"Perhaps you have a picture of her wearing it?"

John answered, "Yes…but she doesn't have anything else on with it."

"I see. Maggie is waiting for you in the conference room."

She smiled at John when he walked in. John once again had to control his urge to embrace and kiss her.

"John, I was so excited when Dr. Roberts told me you were coming to visit me."

"I have a present for you."

She reminded him of a child at Christmas as she opened up the houndstooth gift bag.

"You brought me Ghirardelli candy and what's this—oh, my—what a lovely book."

"It's a sketchbook."

On the cover of the sketchbook was a vintage Victorian Pre-Raphaelite painting featuring a mermaid brushing her long raven hair by the seashore. John had brought back a print of it to her when he had visited the Royal Academy of Arts in London. Maggie had it framed and hung it over her bed.

"How did you know she's my favorite mermaid? John William Waterhouse did this painting in 1900."

To John's pleasant surprise, Maggie gave him a hug and a peck on his cheek.

"But...But, I don't have anything to give you."

"That isn't necessary. It makes me happy to give these to you. Hey, do you have a new outfit on?"

John had sent Mary money for her to buy clothes for Maggie to wear.

"Yes. Mary brought me several outfits that they let me wear. A little conservative for my taste, but much better than the scrubs I was wearing. At least, you can tell I'm a girl."

"I don't think anybody could ever mistake you for a guy."

"Can you tell me how I know you? You live in San Francisco, and I live in Gulf Shores in the cottage you told me about. How did we meet?"

"We met at the Atlanta Airport."

"An airport, but I'm afraid to fly. I can't stand heights."

"I know that."

"Tell me something else that you know about me, something that a stranger would not know."

"There are so many things I know about you. You have a beautiful butterfly tattoo."

Maggie wrinkled her face and replied, "How do you know that?"

205

"I was with you when you got it."

Unfortunately, Dr. Roberts came in and interrupted them. "Maggie, it's time to say goodbye"

John thought, *Damn it. If only they'd let me talk more to her.*

Sarcastically, Maggie said, "Yes, goodbye, Dr. Roberts."

Dr. Roberts replied, "Nice try, Maggie, but you know we keep a tight schedule here."

John hated leaving her; he tried to sound upbeat. "Maggie, I'm looking forward to meeting with you again soon. Perhaps you'll show me some sketches you've done when I come back."

Maggie said, "Please don't leave. I'll miss you."

John's heart was aching as he wished he could take her back with him now. He said, "I understand that Wednesday afternoon is open for visitation. I'll see you then."

Dr. Roberts said, "John, would you mind if I walk with you to your car?"

"Not at all. Goodbye, Maggie."

As they walked out of the building Dr. Roberts said, "John, I can tell Maggie is starting to like you. The last thing she needs is to have another relationship go awry. You must be careful that you don't lead her on."

"I'm not intending to lead her on. I care for her immensely; in fact, I love her."

"But the question remains John, will she love you when she regains her memory?"

"I'm willing to take that chance."

Dr. Roberts nodded his head. "We have to be very cautious at this stage."

John couldn't wait to see Maggie again. It was such a beautiful spring day; he asked Dr. Roberts if he could take Maggie for a walk around the grounds. Maggie met John in the reception area. John greeted her with a hug.

"I brought you something today. I know they won't let you have your cell phone and how much you must miss listening to music, so I brought you this iPod. I downloaded some iTunes music on it for you."

"I've wanted one of these for a long time, but you don't need to bring me a gift when you see me. Your company is a special treat in itself."

"It must sometimes get boring for you here."

Maggie squeezed John's hand. "You must see the drawings I did in my new sketchbook. Let's sit on a bench outside."

They sat on a wooden park bench in front of a fountain. Maggie said, "This is where I like to sit and draw."

"I can see why; it's pleasant here. Now show me your sketches."

As she handed him her sketchbook, she said, "I'm afraid I've gotten a little rusty; they're not that good."

John smiled as he looked at the first drawing of the sunflowers he'd given her.

"You're too modest. These sunflowers are lovely."

Maggie returned his smile, "Thank you. I'm glad you like them."

John viewed her second drawing. "Your butterfly tattoo." *Which looks almost identical to the painting she gave me for my birthday.*

"I hope you're not offended by these next drawings. I like to draw nude figures. I've been having these dreams, and these are sketches of them."

John was overwhelmed. The first one was similar to the first scene of the *Metamorphosis* painting Maggie did. As in the painting, Maggie was nude on the beach near the rocks, with waves crashing. Unlike in her painting, her face was turned away, looking into the water where a body was floating face down.

207

The second sketch was similar to her mermaid in the grotto painting, but the human appeared to be dead in the arms of the main mermaid who was crying. The other mermaids outside the grotto were also crying. Maggie said, "Have you read Hans Christian Andersen's *The Little Mermaid*?" Maggie rubbed her scar. "He wrote that mermaids have no tears and, therefore, they suffer more. Do you like that I'm letting them cry?"

John didn't know quite what to say. "Crying can be therapeutic. What's the last time you remember crying?"

"When my mother punished me for something bad I did."

"Do you like mermaids?"

"Yes, I do. I have a really neat statue of one somewhere. It was the only thing that I found when Hurricane Ivan destroyed our beach house."

"Have you shared your sketches with anyone?"

"No, I want you to have these. They're my present to you."

"Thank you. I will cherish them. Let's go for a walk. You can show me around."

When John got home, he studied Maggie's last two sketches for hours trying to understand their meaning. He sent an email to Dr. Roberts, who emailed back asking John to scan and send them to him. After Dr. Roberts had received them, he emailed he would like to talk to John on the phone the next day.

"John, thanks for agreeing to talk to me today. I hope I didn't inconvenience you?"

"Not at all, Dr. Roberts."

"Please, you can call me, Mike, when I'm not around my patients."

"Alright, Mike. As I told you last night, these sketches were similar to two paintings that Maggie has painted since I've known her. She claimed they were images from her recent dreams. The one showing her on the beach with a body floating in the ocean was similar to her painting *Metamorphosis*, which included three different timelines. I photographed her one afternoon when we were exploring the beach. She used my photographs to compose her painting."

"Can you describe this painting in more detail?

"The first scene is symbolic of her past. She is nude on the beach, near the rocks and crashing waves. She looks distant and sad; she is erotically touching herself, still imprisoned by her past."

"Let me interrupt you; is Sean her past?"

"Precisely. The second scene is symbolic of the present and captures her lying on a blanket after we made love.

"The third scene is a rite of passage. The sun is setting. She's in a trance-like state at the edge of the water kneeling down, letting go of the demons of her past."

Dr. Roberts remarked, "It's interesting that she only drew the first timeline, don't you think?"

"And why she added a drowned man to the scene."

"Tell me about her next sketch."

"Again, it's similar to another painting of hers from Gulf Shores. She has a real fondness for mermaids. She even has a grotto design theme in her bedroom. Her older painting suggests that the mortal is abducting the mermaids. In Maggie's sketch, the mortal is dead, and the mermaids are crying."

Dr. Roberts said, "Perhaps another vision of Sean's death. John, I think she's telling us something important in these sketches. I need to ask her more questions. Perhaps this is the link we've been looking for."

"I think so too. But if you question her, knowing Maggie, she will be angry that I shared them with you without her permission. I don't want to betray her trust. Can I question her about this? You can watch and stop me at any time."

Dr. Roberts asked, "When can you come?"
"How about tomorrow afternoon?

CHAPTER TWENTY-THREE

MAGGIE'S ESCAPE FROM ALCATRAZ

Sitting in a chair, Maggie dangled her long legs as she anxiously waited for John in the conference room.

"Maggie, it's so good to see you again. I brought you more chocolate."

"John, are you trying to make me fat?"

"If you don't want them, I can always take them back."

She raised her right eyebrow. "Did I say I didn't want them?"

"Look what I did with your sketches?"

"You put them in an album."

"They are so good, I didn't want them to get wrinkled or smudged. Although I can't draw like you Maggie, I love to take photographs."

"You do? What do you like to photograph?"

"Pretty girls like you."

"You're funny. Can you keep a secret?"

"Of course."

"When I was in college I used to be a life model. Do you know what that is?"

"Someone who poses nude for artists or photographers."

"Can you believe that I did that?"

"You have nothing to be ashamed of; the human body is a beautiful thing."

"Would you ever photograph someone nude?"

"Only with their permission."

"I've never had anyone photograph me like that before. I guess it wouldn't be much different than posing for an art class."

"I have some questions for you about your sketches. When I take photographs, I hope they will either tell a story or share my emotions with the person who views them. In your mermaid picture, why are the mermaids crying?"

"They're crying because the mortal they love is dead. The mermaids outside the grotto are blaming the mermaid holding his body for killing him."

"What were your thoughts when you sketched this woman on the beach?"

"She's all alone now and sad."

"Who is that man in the water?"

"Her lover. Someone killed him and threw his body in the ocean."

"Which ocean? Is it the Gulf of Mexico where you live?"

Maggie shook her head, "No. It's too rocky to be the Gulf; I'm not sure where it is."

"Maggie, I know where that beach is."

"How do you know that?"

"Because, I went there with you."

"Could you take me there again?"

"We would have to get permission from Dr. Roberts."

"No, we don't. I checked in here of my own free will, and I can check out at any time. I want to go there with you."

"I don't want anything to interfere with you getting better."

Maggie defensively folded her arms. "John, I'm not some innocent child, which is the way they treat me here. I realize something traumatic must have happened to make me forget the last seven years of my life. Look, I'm tired of being protected like a fragile object that everyone is afraid might break. Take me to this beach."

"I'll discuss this with Dr. Roberts."

Dr. Roberts came in and asked Maggie, "Would you like to ask John if he would care to join you for dinner tonight?"

Maggie turned back to John. The thought of him staying for dinner had brightened her mood. "They're having one of my favorite meals tonight, pizza. They get them from a local restaurant. Can you stay?"

John replied, "I would love to. But if you don't mind, I'd like to talk to Dr. Roberts first. Could you wait for me by the fountain?"

"Mike, you saw what happened. She wants me to take her to that spot on the beach. What should I do?"

"I wish I could give you an easy answer, but cases like Maggie's are unique in how each patient responds to the reintroduction of their past. It seems to be important to her."

"Then I want to take her there. Can we do it tomorrow?"

"John, you seem as anxious as she is."

"I feel totally responsible for what's happened to her. She means the world to me. I have to help her through this."

Maggie was excited when John told her at dinner that he would take her to that special beach tomorrow. John would pick her up around ten in the morning.

As I drive to Santa Rosa, I'm wondering if I'm doing the right thing. I think about when I told Mike how much I loved Maggie, and he posed an important question, "Will she love you when she regains her memory?"

John's somber mood changed the second he saw Maggie's radiant face. "Thank you for getting Dr. Roberts to allow me to do this. Sometimes I feel he's part of the Gestapo."

"I love how you dramatize. Maggie, if you want me to bring you back at any time, just let me know. I thought we would stop at this store along the way and get some things for our picnic."

On their way to the Bodega Country Store, John pointed out the schoolhouse where they filmed *The Birds*.

Maggie said, "That was one of the scariest movies I remember seeing."

Inside the store John asked, "Would you like to pick out some things for our picnic?"

"You go ahead; I want to look at all this Hitchcock memorabilia. We studied about him in a film class I took at Alabama."

When John was ready to check out, he went over to Maggie and asked her, "What would you like to drink?"

"Since it's a picnic, I think wine would be nice."

"I'm not sure about that; Dr. Roberts may not approve."

"The last I heard, legally I'm old enough to drink. Also, I'm not on any medications."

"This will be our secret."

Maggie lifted her chin slightly up and smugly said, "My lips are sealed."

How he wished he could kiss her now. He had selected the same Pinot Noir he'd purchased on their last trip there.

They drove north on the Pacific Coast Highway and stopped at the head of Bodega Bay. John said, "Let's get out. If we're lucky we may still see some gray whales migrating south. Let me get my binoculars so we can look."

Maggie said, "Wow! This view is awesome! Mother Nature paints the best landscapes."

John handed her the binoculars. "Look through these. I see some whales over there."

"Oh yes, I can see them. Did you know the gray whale migrates further than any other mammal on Earth?"

John was caught off guard. "Maggie, you remembered me telling you that from the last time we were here."

Maggie shook her head in disbelief. "I did? I was here with you? That makes me happy."

John put his arm around her and tenderly squeezed her. "Me too, Maggie. Me too. Are you ready to head to the beach?"

Maggie hugged John like a frightened child. "I confess, I'm a little nervous."

John took in the warmth of her body. "Just remember what I said earlier, we can go back at any time."

"No. This is important to me. Please kiss me."

John's willpower failed him. As he tenderly kissed her, his groins ached for her and Maggie felt his hardness. He wanted to ravish her right then, but his conscience told him he would be taking advantage of her; he needed to stop, so he pulled abruptly away.

Maggie said, "Hopefully, I didn't forget how to kiss."

"I'm sorry; that was totally inappropriate of me."

John drove to the highway pull-off and parked in the same spot as he had on that January twenty-second, Sunday afternoon. Like then, the parking area was empty. "It looks like we have the beach to ourselves again."

"I guess not many people come here this time of the year."

"Summer is when it gets busy. Are you ready to hike down? You probably want to put your jacket on; it's chilly by the water. If you'll take the tote bag, I'll bring the cooler."

"Don't you want to take your camera? It's in the back seat. I can get it for you."

He recalled her asking him a similar question when they came there before. "Sure. Let's take it with us."

They hiked to the sheltered spot and spread the blanket down. It was after noon already.

"Let's celebrate my escape from Alcatraz and open the wine."

"You've a wonderful sense of humor." John handed her a bottle of water. "Drink this first."

"Why do you always worry about me being dehydrated?"

John recalled another voice from the past. "I enjoy worrying about you."

"I don't need this jacket. If I were home right now, I would be sunning in my bikini on the beach. Since there's no one around, I'm going to get some sun."

Maggie stood up and pulled off her jeans and pullover shirt revealing her lavender bra and matching panties.

"Glad I wore matching underwear today." Maggie turned around and lowered her bikini panties down so that her butterfly tattoo was in full view. "So, you remember when I got this tattoo?"

"Maggie!"

"John, don't look embarrassed. I've already figured out that you've seen me undressed before. I just wish I could remember what you looked like undressed, but I can imagine you look really sexy."

"Why do you think I've seen you undressed before?"

"Because I have these dreams at night."

"What do you dream?"

"You know…that we're together."

"Intimately together?"

"Extremely intimately together."

John thought it wise to change the subject. "How about some wine and cheese?"

"Are you embarrassed by what I just said?"

"Always feel that you can tell me anything. I care about you."

Maggie held up her empty water bottle, "Finished; would love some wine now."

John opened the bottle of Pinot Noir and poured it into the wine glasses he had brought from home. He plated the goat cheese, crackers, and fresh strawberries.

Maggie picked up the wine bottle and stared at the bottle's label. "How did you know I love this wine?"

John thought this wine was produced in 2011, how would she remember it? He quickly changed the conversation. He could tell Maggie had lost weight, which concerned him.

"Do you realize you've lost weight?"

"I can't stand the food they serve. It's much too healthy. I'm craving a burger and fries."

"On the way back, I know a great place where you can get one. It's called Nick's Cove."

"That would be great. Did you get a tattoo with me that day?"

"As a matter of fact, I did."

"I showed you mine, so you have to show me yours. If you don't show it to me, I'll find it myself. And I warn you, I'll not stop until I find it."

"Alright, I give up. Let me roll down the waist of my jeans."

"I can unfasten them for you if you like?"

John thought, *I know you can,* as he unfastened and rolled them slightly down.

"Lie back so I can see it better."

While propped up on her elbow sideways, Maggie studied John's inked skin. Taking the tip of her pointer finger, she followed the tattoo's outline, something she had done many times before.

"I really like it. It's unique. Δ 211. I know this probably sounds silly, but it reminds me of a Delta airline flight. What does it really mean?"

At that moment John was perplexed; was Maggie just good at guessing or might she be regaining her memory.

"It was a Delta flight. We were both scheduled on it when we first met."

"How long have we known each other?"

"This past January was a year."

"I sense we've known each other longer."

"I wish we had."

After a long pause of silence, John said, "If we're going to get something to eat before we head back, we probably should leave shortly."

"Before we leave, will you take some photos of me?"

"You need to put your clothes back on."

"Why? Remember… I used to be a live model."

"I'm sure you were a stunning model."

"I still am, watch me."

Before John could object, Maggie had run down to the edge of the water leaving a trail of underwear behind. She was wading in the rough water as John ran towards her.

"This water is freezing."

He yelled out, "Maggie no…don't go in…the water is way too rough…there are riptides."

 Before he could reach the edge of the water, Maggie dove into the rough water and was caught in a strong current. John's adrenaline kicked in as he ran along the shoreline, dove into the surf, swimming with all his might towards her. He finally reached her, towing her back to the shore. When she started coughing up water, John felt this enormous relief. He would never be able to live with himself if she had drowned.

"Let's get you to the sheltered area where it's warmer."

John picked her up and carried her to the blanket. He removed a beach towel from the tote bag and said, "Wrap this around you."

"Thank you, Professor."

Overwhelmed, John replied, "You just called me, Professor."

"And I remember why I gave you that name."

"You're freezing; let's put your clothes back on. I need to take you back; I'm sure Dr. Roberts will want to talk to you."

"Dr. Roberts can wait. All I want to do is make love to you at Nick's Cove."

"You need to get dressed."

"My underwear is all sandy now. I'll skip wearing them. But look at you. Your clothes are soaking wet. You need to take them off and wrap the other towel around you."

John turned away from her and took off his wet jeans and Henley shirt and wrapped the towel around his waist.

Maggie said, "Don't be so shy; I remember how well hung you are. Here, you may want to put on your jacket."

"Thanks. I keep sweats in the car, in case I get motivated to go for a run."

"Of course. I remember how you're always prepared for any change in events. Like that Sunday afternoon at the Atlanta Airport when Delta flight 211 was delayed and ..."

"Let's get you dressed; I need to take you back."

"No. We can go back tomorrow. I want to make love to you all night long. Kiss me."

John felt an overwhelming passion he had never felt before. He had almost lost her to another man and now he had almost lost her to the sea.

"I'm horny now. Let's go to your car and make love there."

"Your memory and libido have indeed come back. But we both need warm clothes. Why don't we see if Nick's Cove has our place available for tonight? We'll be much more comfortable there."

"Can we also order the lobster mac and cheese?"

"Maggie O', you can have anything your heart desires. We just need to let everyone know that your memory is back and that you'll see them tomorrow."

"Professor, I like when you call me Maggie O'."

CHAPTER TWENTY-FOUR
MELIADES

Maggie and John arrived at the Memory Institute just in time for their eleven o'clock appointment. Dr. Roberts began by asking John to describe what had happened the previous day. After John finished, Dr. Roberts asked him to allow them to talk to Maggie privately.

Dr. Jim said, "Maggie, we're pleased that you're regaining your memory. But we need to know why you dove into the ocean yesterday; you could have easily drowned."

"I thought someone was calling me."

Dr. Roberts said, "Did you think it was Sean?"

Maggie looked puzzled. "Who is Sean? Why do you keep mentioning him to me?"

Dr. Jim replied, "He was important to you in your past."

Dr. Roberts took a chance and asked her, "Was Sharon calling you?"

"No. Sharon was killed by a DUI driver."

Her memory of Sharon had returned.

Dr. Jim replied, "Yes, I'm sorry you lost your friend."

Dr. Roberts said, "Maggie, what do you do for a living?"

"I'm a partner in an art gallery in New York and I also oversee the Art Heals Cancer Foundation."

Dr. Roberts continued. "I know you and John have a lot of catching up to do, but it's important that we help you regain all of your memory back. The sooner this happens, the sooner you'll be able to live a normal life again. We would like for you to consider staying here a little while longer."

"Why? I don't understand?"

"You still haven't fully recovered your memory."

"I'll compromise, stay here during the week, but I want to be with John on the weekends."

John was not happy when Dr. Jim told him that Maggie was still suppressing her memory of Sean.

"Before yesterday Maggie had continuous dissociative amnesia, meaning her amnesia covered the entire seven-year period from when she met Sean to the present. Now it has changed to systematized amnesia since it only relates to her memory of Sean."

"So doctors, what are your plans now?"

Dr. Roberts said, "Continuing psychotherapy and encouraging her to continue to draw her sketches. But we also think we should consider a more controversial treatment, sodium amytal."

John asked, "Isn't sodium amytal a so-called, truth serum?"

"That's correct. Jim and I have both seen success from its use in similar cases."

"Then why is it considered controversial?"

"There is a risk of creating false memories," Dr. Jim replied.

"Before you try such controversial treatment, I have an idea you may consider. I have a painting she did when she and Sean were living together. She painted it from a photograph he took of her. Perhaps it will bring back her early memories of him. It's rather large, so it would be difficult for me to bring it here. You could take her to my place."

Dr. Roberts said, "Maggie has already put a condition of her continuing treatment that she has the weekends available to stay with you."

"I must warn you, the painting is erotic."

Dr. Jim said, "Maggie could withdraw further when she sees it, but I think it's worth the risk; what's your opinion, Mike?"

"I say we take the risk. I believe artists are uniquely wired; I married one. But I won't be available until the following weekend to go."

Jim turned to John. "I'm staying at Steve's in the Soma district this weekend. I could bring Maggie to your place this Friday around four."

"That's perfect. I live in the Pacific Heights district on Vallejo Street. I'll write down my address."

Maggie was excited to be spending the weekend with John. They had not discussed the portrait she would be viewing. On the way to John's, Dr. Jim asked her several questions concerning the art she had painted.

"John tells me you're a talented artist and that he has several of your paintings."

"He has them hung in his New York apartment. They're quite risqué; he doesn't want the twins to see them."

"Do you get along with his twins?"

"I've never met them. They go to a boarding school in Switzerland. John wants me to go with them on their summer vacation this year. They're renting a house in the Abaco Islands."

"Dr. Roberts takes his family there. Tell me more about your art. Have you done any art shows before?"

"Just the one I did of Sharon for the New Hope Clinic."

"Nothing prior to that?"

"Well, I don't count the shows I had to do in college."

John waited anxiously for Dr. Jim and Maggie to arrive. He studied *Meliades*, the fifty-five-inch by eighty-five-inch painting displayed in his bedroom. He suddenly felt jealous imagining her as Sean's muse back then, how they lived together and traveled the world together. Then he remembered hearing about the dark side of this man and how dangerously abusive he was towards her, whether it was drugging her or performing erotic asphyxiation. And then, how he charmed his way back into her life because he needed her money.

Maggie's heart started racing as John opened the door for them to come in. She gave John a hug and wished that Dr. Jim would hurry up and leave.

John said, "Please come in. I've made some espresso and picked up some chocolate croissants from b. patisserie."

"When did you start making espresso and eating chocolate croissants? Dr. Jim, I think we're in the wrong place."

"The twins gave me an espresso cappuccino maker for Christmas. Maggie, why don't you show Jim around while I get everything ready?"

"Alright. The painting here in the foyer is of me sunbathing in Puerto Vallarta. My friend, Sharon, painted it. We spent her last New Years there. I miss her."

Jim replied, "She was a special friend."

As they walked into the living room, Maggie continued, "John is a talented photographer. He took all of these black and white photographs."

John walked in carrying a tray, "Maggie, show Jim the painting you did in the bedroom."

"There's a painting I did in the bedroom? I thought the paintings you bought are in your New York condo?"

John put the tray down on the cocktail table and said, "Let's go into the bedroom, and I will show you."

Both John and Jim closely observed Maggie as she viewed her painting. For several minutes, she was both speechless and motionless, in a catatonic state.

Jim said, "Maggie do you remember painting this?"

Tears formed in her eyes. "He's dead because of me. I should have told him not to go. But there was this conflict inside me."

Jim said, "What kind of conflict?"

"I was still stuck in my fairy tale beliefs about love, running off to Pantelleria to get married."

Maggie looked over to John and said. "But what I really was running from was another relationship. I had been betrayed by another man I truly love."

Jim said, "Maggie, I can take you back to Santa Rosa now. Perhaps this was not a good idea."

John interrupted Jim, "Maggie, believe me when I tell you, I never willingly betrayed you. My only crime was having a drink in the wrong place at the wrong time. I had bought you a platinum and diamond engagement ring that day at the Cartier store and I was showing it off to my friend. Evidently, this prostitute was watching us. She came over and sat next to me at the bar and commented on how nice a ring I had. When I came to, in my hotel room the next day, the ring was gone, along with my other belongings. The police caught her doing the same thing to another businessman several weeks ago. I have the police report to prove it."

Maggie said, "So you were going to ask me to marry you?"

"Yes. I love you. I had this plan all figured out how we both could continue our careers and still be married. We would both make New York our main base for work. And still keep our two other residences for business use and pleasure. I was going to order you another ring to replace the one that was robbed; I'd rather take you shopping for it."

Maggie turned to Dr. Jim and said, "Would you mind leaving now? John is taking me shopping."

As they stood in front of the ring display case at the Cartier store on Grant Street, John said, "Maggie, are you sure you don't want an engagement ring?"

Maggie had insisted on matching simple platinum wedding bands. "I like the simplicity of wearing just a band."

To make it more personalized John had them engrave Δ 211 on the inside.

"Then I really want to give you an engagement gift. What about these pearl and diamond earrings? They would look great when you wear your pearl necklace and pearl thong."

"I gave the choker to Mary."

"Why?"

"Bad memories; It had belonged to my mother."

John said, "Changing the subject, we need to decide on a date."

"Your travel schedule is crazy, and I have several more commissions to do."

"Let's get married in Atlanta with your friends and family when I get back from my trip and we can fly to Switzerland and see the twins."

"What about Saturday before Memorial Day? Colin will be out of school then."

Samuel was waiting for them when they landed in Atlanta. John had previously contacted him with specific wedding instructions. He first stopped at the Fulton County Probate Court so they could get a marriage license.

Back in the limo, Maggie said, "I can't believe how easy that was. Are you sure you still want to go through with this?"

"Honestly, Maggie, if you ask me that one more time I'm going to have to punish you on our wedding night."

Samuel pulled up to the Gospel Baptist Church and chuckled. "Miss Maggie, you'll have a shotgun wedding if Mr. Kramer tries to back out now."

"Samuel, I brought a special dress I'd like to change into before the ceremony."

Just in time for the ceremony to start, Maggie's half-brother, Colin, and her stepmother sat down next to Matthew and Mary on the front row pew. Wearing his finest black cassock, the Reverend Samuel stood at the altar singing along with his niece as she played *Amazing Grace* on the spinet organ. At the end of the song, John entered from the side door and anxiously stood next to Samuel. Maggie and her father appeared at the back of the church, and Samuel nodded for his niece to begin playing *Ave Maria.*

Escorted by her father, Maggie walked down the center aisle wearing a Tadashi Shoji black lace and mesh cap over John's favorite red dress. She held a fragrant gardenia nosegay.

Matthew whispered to Mary, "At least she is wearing something over that red dress."

Mary replied, "I should have gotten rid of it when I had a chance."

As Maggie stood next to John exchanging vows, she realized she had finally found her soul mate after fourteen years of searching.

With a broad smile on his face, The Reverend Samuel said, "Therefore, it's my pleasure, that I pronounce Mr. Kramer and Miss Maggie, husband and wife." Turning to John he continued, "Mr. Kramer, you may now kiss your bride."

Following the wedding, Maggie, John, Mary, and Matthew enjoyed a four-course dinner with wine pairings at Bacchanalia, Maggie's favorite Atlanta restaurant. They sat downstairs in the cozy, candlelit wine cellar and were the last ones to leave the restaurant. Samuel drove them all back to the Ritz. John thanked Samuel for all he had done with a $5,000 tip.

John kissed her the entire elevator ride up. When the elevator door opened, he scooped her up. Maggie said, "What are you doing?"

"I'm going to carry you over the threshold." John had reserved his favorite suite, room 2423 at the Ritz Carlton. "And then make love to you until we have to leave for Switzerland tomorrow afternoon."

Once inside the room, John put Maggie down, removed her cape, and reached into his jacket pocket, "I have a wedding gift for you." He handed her a red velvet jewelry box.

Maggie opened the hinged box and pulled out a 58-inch strand of Mikimoto pearls. "John, these are exquisite."

"Hand them to me."

John looped them around her neck; the long ends dangled down the center of her back. As he leaned against her backside, he had several erotic ideas of how he would have her wear them.

Maggie moaned as his hands cupped her breasts.

He said, I'd like to discuss something important with you."

"Can it wait? I'm so aroused."

"The doctor said my vasectomy reversal procedure has a 44% chance of success."

Maggie turned towards him and placed her arms around his neck. "I like playing games of chance; don't you?"

John backed her up against the wall until their bodies were meshed together.

Maggie lowered his trouser zipper. "I know several things I can do to increase our chances."

"Maggie O', you're such a hot tease."

As she dropped to her knees, Maggie replied, "And you wouldn't have it any other way, Professor."

ABOUT THE AUTHOR

Pamela Boleyn is a former financial executive, living on the Eastern Shore of Alabama. A hopeless romantic, she intertwines her Southern roots with her passion for art, cooking, and travel into her vivid stories. *Maggie O', Seven Years Forgotten* is her first published novel. Currently, she is working on her next novel *Scarlett's Revenge* for Boleyn Books.

You can contact Pamela through her website, www.boleynbooks.com.

Made in the USA
Columbia, SC
10 January 2020